"Aren't you going to look at my tongue?"

Rafe asked Kat, pushing himself up in bed.

"Aren't you going to take my temperature?" he persisted as she opened her bag. "Where's the bedside manner doctors are famous for?"

"To begin with, I'm not a doctor—"

"We've been through that before. Let's get back to the bedside manner."

"Vets don't need one." Kat touched his forehead. It was hot. She took a rolled-up towel from her bag. "Put this on your chest."

"On my chest?" Rafe could have thought of worse things, and from the flush on Kat's cheeks, he had a feeling this was going to be interesting. "What do I have to do?"

"Just take off your pajama top."

"With pleasure, my lady," Rafe murmured after a beat, reaching for the buttons.

"Rafe!" Kat blushed in spite of herself. "You know what I mean. And I'm not your *lady!*"

Dear Reader,

It's February—the month of love! And what better way to celebrate St. Valentine's Day than with Silhouette Romance.

Silhouette Romance novels always reflect the magic of love in compelling stories that will make you laugh and cry and move you time and time again. This month is no exception. Our heroines find happiness with the heroes of their dreams—from the boy next door to the handsome, mysterious stranger. We guarantee their heartwarming stories of love will delight you.

February continues our WRITTEN IN THE STARS series. Each month in 1992, we're proud to present a book that focuses on the hero and his astrological sign. This month we're featuring the adventurous Aquarius man in the enchanting *The Kat's Meow* by Lydia Lee.

In the months to come, watch for Silhouette Romance books by your all-time favorites such as Diana Palmer, Suzanne Carey, Annette Broadrick, Brittany Young and many, many more. The Silhouette Romance authors and editors love to hear from readers, and we'd love to hear from *you*.

Happy Valentine's Day...and happy reading!

Valerie Susan Hayward
Senior Editor

LYDIA LEE

The Kat's Meow

Silhouette Romance

Published by Silhouette Books New York

America's Publisher of Contemporary Romance

For Ozzie Green and the miracle of love he gives me.

With thanks to:
Shirley Ellis, Samantha Hancock, Susanne and
Matt Kalen, Mary Kilchenstein, Bill Walsh,
Kevin Reilly, DVM, and the staff of the
Manakin Veterinarian Clinic.

SILHOUETTE BOOKS
300 E. 42nd St., New York, N.Y. 10017

THE KAT'S MEOW

Copyright © 1992 by Lydia Lee

LOVE AND THE AQUARIUS MAN
Copyright © 1992 by Harlequin Enterprises B.V.

ISBN: 0-373-08844-2

First Silhouette Books printing February 1992

Printed in the U.S.A.

Books by Lydia Lee

Silhouette Romance

Valentino's Pleasure #642
Thank Your Lucky Stars #784
The Kat's Meow #844

LYDIA LEE

Astrology has fascinated me ever since I can remember. Being told in childhood that I was a dramatic and headstrong Leo wasn't enough—the Lion's profile didn't completely fit me. It wasn't until I was grown that I learned how a Scorpio Moon and a Pisces Rising could change all that! This knowledge helped explain my occasional lapses into shyness (hardly a Leo trait). But more than that, it lured me into studying astrology. Suddenly I started seeing why seemingly incompatible signs sang such sweet music together. Several years later when I began writing romances, astrology was a big inspiration. When Silhouette initiated WRITTEN IN THE STARS, I was like a kid in a candy store: the possibilities were endless! I still occasionally cast charts, but most of my time is spent creating wonderful love stories. For despite modern-day cynicism, romance *is* alive and well, and there *are* real-life happy endings.

AQUARIUS

Eleventh sign of the Zodiac
January 21 to February 19
Symbol: Water Bearer
Planet: Uranus
Element: Air
Stone: Amethyst
Color: Blue
Metal: Lead, Uranium
Flower: Violet
Lucky Day: Saturday
Countries: USSR, Sweden, Canada
Cities: Hamburg, Salzberg, Leningrad

Famous Aquarians

Abraham Lincoln
Clark Gable
Paul Newman
James Dean

Oprah Winfrey
Farrah Fawcett
Lana Turner
Eartha Kitt

Prologue

"According to the stars, my granddaughter and your nephew make the match in heaven, *sì?*" Rosa Motta pressed the astrology charts to her ample bosom, then with a fluttery sigh placed them on the marble-topped coffee table that lay between herself and her friend, Mimi Chandler.

"Celestial powers will indeed bring them together, with a little help from us," Mimi murmured in agreement as she poured them both steaming cups of chamomile tea. "However," she added, handing Rosa her tea, "from what you've told me about your granddaughter, she mustn't suspect that we're assisting in this match."

Rosa winked a mischievous brown eye. "We've got a foolproof plot. My little Katrina and your little—"

"Not so little." Mimi laughed. "Rafe is six feet tall and unfortunately, unpredictable. But...that's an Aquarian for you."

Rosa nodded sympathetically. "Kat's not so perfect, either. A Leo with Virgo rising! *Dio mio.* But she makes a good veterinarian. Still, this work, work, work—this is not so good.''

"And it's going to change," Mimi assured her as she lifted the delicate porcelain cup to her lips for a sip of tea. Then both women fell into a companionable silence.

Ever since Mimi Chandler, a silver-haired dowager who believed you could never be too thin or too rich, joined the Pineboro County Metaphysical Society, she and Rosa Motta had become best friends. An incongruous friendship, for although both women were widows in their mid-sixties, they came from very different backgrounds: Mimi was a member of old Richmond society and reeked of equally old money; Rosa was from the Old Country, and usually reeked of garlic from the highly successful *ristorante* she and her husband had started forty years ago. She spoke with an Italian accent, and when she got excited she spoke Italian.

Rosa was short, plump, dark-eyed and merry. Her salt-and-pepper hair was twisted into a bun on the back of her neck; she wore chunky gold jewelry, complemented by colorful caftans that added to her aura as founder and past president of the Pineboro Metaphysical Society. She was a great believer in communing with nature, and frequently went barefoot.

Mimi thought this quaint, though *her* size-four feet were also shod in the very finest leather. Everything about Mimi was coordinated, matching and elegant, yet neither woman seemed to find their mutual interest in the occult at odds with their everyday lives. Nor did they think it strange that they had become such comrades in arms.

Mimi set down her teacup with precision, then picking up the astrology charts said, "Katrina's Moon on Rafe's Sun is quite divine, not to mention that lovely trine of Mars and Venus." A single, plucked eyebrow arched triumphantly as she wickedly added, "Cupid's delight!"

"*Grazie a Dio!* And to Cupid, Venus, St. Anthony and St. Jude. They are all behind our plan, for it's just what Kat needs. After all, it's been more than a year since the death of her husband, and though everyone tells her it was not her fault, do you think she listens? I tell her to go out and meet some people, some nice man, and always she says, 'Later, Nana.'"

With a shrug of her shoulders, Rosa poured them both more tea and continued. "But, as you say, all of this will change. In Napoli there is a saying that fate is like the wind—it can change in the blinking of the eye."

"And we're simply helping those winds along, giving fate a gentle pat in the right direction." Mimi drew her lips together in a slow smile, then declining Rosa's offer of another piece of cake, murmured a compliment on it nevertheless.

Rosa grinned back. Both ladies were delighted that the Metaphysical Society's monthly meeting had ended early so they could get down to the business at hand: the matching of their unsuspecting relations. The heavy fog that had rolled into the Richmond area on the heels of a February heat wave had led the ladies of the Pineboro Metaphysical to quickly conclude their discussion of parallel past lives. They'd left Rosa's Georgian farmhouse, leaving in their wake the remains of the heart-shaped, fuchsia-iced, double fudge cake. The hasty inroads made on the dessert left it looking like a piece of modern art that belonged on the wall along with the rest of Rosa's eclectic collection.

Mimi, about to speak, paused as a cuckoo clock announced the hour. She gazed up at a print of Salvadore Dalí's melting watches and said, "Timing is everything, and frankly, I think we couldn't have picked a better time to bring these two together than at Rafe's surprise birthday party."

"*And* on Valentine's Day!" Rosa reminded her as her gaze wandered to the remains of the heart-shaped cake. Then, reaching for another slice, she gleefully tacked on, "And it's his thirtieth birthday, which means he's probably finishing up his Saturn return!" This pronouncement was made as an astrological benediction on the entire affair, ensuring its success, and allowing Rosa to give her attention to the forkful of fuchsia and chocolate about to enter her mouth.

Mimi let out a sigh and somewhat reluctantly said, "Yes, it's giving him quite a workout, but as for learning Saturn's lesson, I'm afraid Rafe is resisting it with everything he's got." She paused, then slowly added, "You remember I told you how he and his fiancée called off the wedding last February. Well, since then he's turned into a workaholic—"

"Bravo! So now he'll be ready for a change, he'll be ready for my Katrina, *y per amore!*"

"But my dear, you see, while he's not working, he's been having many *amores.*" At Rosa's puzzled look, Mimi quickly added, "Typically, he's charted a determined bachelor's course, and the only women he dates are these…these *bimbos!* It's not at all like him. Then I suppose it's his Cancer Moon opposing all those Capricorn transits."

"*È già!*" Rosa cried out, putting down her cake. "And it's making him feel torn between work and matters of the heart. But it is time for a change!"

"You know," said Mimi thoughtfully, "I can't help but wonder if nature wouldn't have brought them together anyway."

"Perhaps. Still, we give a little help, *sì?* For I have a feeling that my Katrina is going to come into his life with such a big bang that he won't know what hit him!"

"Gracious, Rosa, isn't that a bit strong? She's not going to jump out of his birthday cake, you know." Contemplating the colorful confection on Rosa's plate, Mimi laughed. "Although, that's not a bad idea."

Gazing at their charts once again, Rosa added, "However they come together, I sense it will be dramatic."

"And with your intuition, you're probably right," Mimi agreed.

Rosa nodded her head; she couldn't have explained the feeling she was having for all the money in the world, but somehow she knew that it really didn't matter what she and Mimi did, because Katrina and Rafe were star-crossed lovers destined to meet. And what an encounter it promised to be!

Chapter One

Rafe was out of his car in a flash. It had been one hell of a flight from O'Hare. They'd had to circle the local airport for an hour. Baggage claim took forever. There was an accident on Patterson Avenue, and here some idiot came zooming out of the fog, cut in front of him—right in his own drive—and... He stopped in his tracks as something in voluminous quantities of turquoise-colored lace jumped out of a dented pickup truck. Was it prom night?

"What the devil did you think you were doing?" Rafe demanded as he moved toward the young woman.

"What was *I* doing?" she snapped back, planting her hands firmly on her hips, fire smoldering in her dark eyes. "You nearly creamed me!" With a wave of her hand she indicated Rafe's M.G.

"*I* nearly creamed *you?*" Throwing his head back, he gave a bark of laughter. "Oh, that's a good one, and I suppose you always cut in front of people in the fog *and* in their own driveways."

This comment quieted the woman for the moment. Rafe could tell she was not, as he'd thought on first seeing the little spitfire, a teenager. She was a woman all right, he realized as the light from his flashlight swept over her, from her stylish cap of dark hair with its crown of white carnations to the tips of her blue satin heels. Although she was petite—he quickly guessed just under five feet—her figure was softly rounded in all the right places. Turquoise looked good on her, he decided. Then, catching himself and pulling his gaze from the luscious expanse of smooth skin her scooped neckline revealed, he reminded himself that she was still a menace on the road. And from the look on her upturned face, one that had no intention of moving.

"I suggest," she began on a protracted indrawn breath, "that you check out your headlights before you go accusing strangers of ramming into you. May I remind you, it was *you* who nearly hit *me!*"

Rafe noticed that only one headlight was on, and it was pretty dim. "Oh," he muttered after a moment. He wanted to add that she should have seen him anyway, but realizing the ridiculousness of that he quietly added, "I'm sorry."

"Apology accepted," she said. Matter-of-factly hitching up the lacy gown and hoisting herself back into the truck, she added, "Your driveway? Then I suppose it's your mare I'm tending to." She flashed him a generous smile as she leaned out the window. "Name's Katrina Racanelli."

"Wait a minute. *You're* tending my mare?" Gripping the truck door handle as if he might hop aboard, Rafe was rewarded with a whiff of her floral fragrance. *Spring: this woman made him think of spring.*

"Yes," she replied in precise tones. "Someone named Marty called me saying Nightstar was going into premature labor, and when I tried to tell him that although I'm a vet, I'm—"

"Get going!" Rafe said, moving toward his car. "She may not be Secretariat, but she's pretty special." Slipping behind the wheel of his M.G., he followed the red truck down the fog-enshrouded curve of graveled driveway. "Kat Racanelli," he muttered to himself, wondering where she'd been at one o'clock in the morning in her chic little number. Undoubtedly she'd been dragged away from a stylish party, which would explain her snippy mood. Good Lord, a socialite vet driving a dented pickup: what a bizarre combination. Some veterinarian she must be, Rafe thought. Why hadn't his brother called Dr. Roberts? Vets were supposed to be men, he thought, reveling in his momentary lapse into Stone Age machismo. What planet had this Dr. Racanelli come from anyway?

Planet, he caught himself. Right. Blame it on the planets. What was that ridiculous horoscope prediction he'd read on the plane? Something about Aquarian men bumping into fiery Leo ladies, and wedding bells in the future? A lot of nonsense as far as Rafe was concerned. And wedding bells? Thanks, but no thanks. He'd be thirty this week, and two of the things for which he would always be most grateful were first, that despite the fact he was born on February 14, his father had talked his mother out of naming him Valentino. Second, and more recent was the fact that those good old wedding bells had *not* tolled for him, at least not yet. Nearly a year ago, he'd almost taken that step when he and his fiancée, auburn-haired socialite Millicent Sydney, had admitted their mistake and called off the wedding. Rafe had decided then and there that he'd had it with women, except as a diversion. Serious relationships made too great an emotional demand on him. Besides, his wealth and position attracted enough women to provide plenty of amusement for his tastes.

Gravel spun off his wheels as he went into the final curve of the drive and came to a stop beside the red truck. Kat Racanelli bounded out, small black bag in hand and an intense air of business about her that was at odds with the ball gown.

"The barn's this way," Rafe said, with more gruffness than he'd intended, but damn it all, this liberated Cinderella was more distracting to him than gopher holes on a golf course.

"I'll follow your beam," the vet replied, falling in step beside him. "By the way, I wouldn't worry too much if I were you. From what Marty said it sounds like a fairly uncomplicated premature birth, less than a week till her due date, although I ought to tell you—"

"That you don't usually wear designer originals on *barn calls?*"

"Very funny," she replied, testiness reappearing in her voice. "What I was about to say is that—oh, damn!"

Rafe jerked around as he felt her hand clamp onto his arm for support. "Are you all right?"

"Of course I'm okay. It's just that I've broken the heel off my shoe." Retaining her grip on Rafe's arm, she bent down and retrieved the remains of her satin slipper, then with a laugh added, "Oh, well, they're only meant to be worn once."

Although Rafe couldn't see her face all that well, from the sound of her voice he suspected she was smiling, as if the joke were on him.

He knew her type, after all; Millicent never wore the same cocktail dress twice in a season. But shoes? That really took the cake. And she was going to deliver Nightstar's foal? Just then the doors to the foaling barn swung open and a block of amber light pierced the mist.

"Hey, Rafe, is that you?" the chipper voice of his half brother, Marty, greeted them.

"With Dr. Racanelli," he answered, quickening his pace and closing the distance between them. Although younger than his brother, Rafe always felt older, but then Martin, having been raised in England in an even foxier set than Pineboro County, Virginia, was the charming, perennial playboy who'd made a harmless career of marrying young debutantes on both sides of the Atlantic.

"Nightstar's holding her own, but it's reassuring to have you here, Dr. Racanelli." Gesturing for Rafe and the veterinarian to enter, Marty quickly led the way down a well-lit passage to the stall where the mare was lying on her side.

Kat slipped into her white lab coat, put a stethoscope around her neck and, kicking off her other shoe, knelt beside the sweating mare. She spoke to her in a soothing voice while she gently palpated the extended belly. "Sometimes Mother Nature needs a little help," she said over her shoulder as she reached into her medical kit for sterile gloves. Then, snapping them on, she added as casually as possible, "So, we'll just see if we can't help things along." After inserting her hand into the birth canal, she could feel the foal's head bearing down. At least Kat wasn't going to have to turn the baby. In fact, after listening to the foal's heartbeat, she probably wasn't going to have to do much of anything, except hold the nervous "father's" hand. Glancing up at Rafe from her crouched position confirmed her suspicion: there was a strained look about his aristocratic features. This was probably his favorite mare.

"What's the prognosis?" he asked in a surprisingly quiet voice as he hunkered down next to Nightstar.

"She's foaled before, hasn't she? Several times?"

"Yes, but how did you—never mind. You're a vet, and you obviously know your stuff."

"Even if I *do* wear formal attire?" she couldn't resist saying as she rocked back on her heels, grateful that the mare was doing fine. She also couldn't resist taking a mildly perverse pleasure in Mr. Sinclair's discomfort.

"You look fetching," Marty interjected, as he pushed away from the stall door and sauntered forward. "However, that white coat isn't really much protection."

"Oh, I doubt I'll wear this outfit any time again soon. Well, not until my other sisters get married. Besides, I'm really not much of a turquoise lace person." Turning back to the mare, who was making audible sounds preparatory to the foal's birth, Kat missed the confused look on both men's faces. She could handle only one thing at a time, and having assisted her husband a few times in foaling, she knew Nightstar needed her full attention. Thankfully, this mama was an old pro, and unless her foal was defective in some way, everything should be fine.

Within minutes a healthy colt with long, skinny legs was born to a proud mare that, knowing immediately what to do, managed to pull herself to an upright position and nudge the foal into a similar attempt. The little fellow, although ungainly, succeeded in standing after the third try, and looking inquisitively at his mother, gave a soft whinny, then began to nurse. Kat sat quietly for several minutes to make sure the initial bonding took place, then feeling a reverence for this touching scene, slowly rose. She backed out of the stall, leaving the Sinclair brothers with the mare and colt.

Thank God there were no complications, she thought, taking a deep breath of crisp night air. The colt was less than a week premature, and from the looks of him, he was fairly sturdy; no doubt the blessings of an excellent mare and stallion. But what if there *had* been complications? There weren't, she reminded herself, stepping farther away from the barn.

The fog had lifted and only a swirl of mist remained, revealing a pale sky, a fat pewter moon and a scattering of distant stars. It could almost be Montana, but Kat had left Montana a year ago. She'd left the Cross Star Ranch and the veterinary practice she and her husband had begun, and left all the pain and all the memories. She'd even thought of starting another career; for every time she looked at an animal, whether it was a cat, a horse or a cow, she thought of Jack and the stable fire that had claimed his life. It also made her face her own guilt. But eventually she had realized that only through continuing her practice would she have any peace at all. Glancing back at the barn she willed the image of that long-ago fire from her thoughts. Perhaps someday it, too, like the fog, would lift, leaving her free and innocent.

"Dr. Racanelli!" Hearing her name jolted her back to the present. She saw Rafe Sinclair moving toward her rather quickly.

"Is everything all right?" she called out, bracing herself for a sudden turn for the worse.

"No problem at all," he replied, coming up to her. "I want to thank you for leaving your sister's wedding reception. Marty explained how he'd reached you, and well, I thought maybe you'd like to have some hot coffee and get warm while we settle up. My brother said he'd stay a few more minutes with Nightstar."

"That's very kind of you, but I really don't—"

"I insist for selfish reasons. You see, it's to soothe my conscience for being a bit of a prig with you earlier. Also I owe you for that broken slipper." Taking her arm as if it were the most ordinary thing in the world, he guided her toward his house.

"Oh, yes. The slipper." Surprising herself with a laugh, Kat added, "My truck might turn into a pumpkin at any moment."

"And the bridesmaid's gown, a tattered dress? We'll have to see about that." His voice had a dark, rich timbre to it, and when Kat looked up at him she saw a distinctively devilish gleam in his oh-so-blue eyes. She felt a prickle of excitement tingle through her veins.

"I really can't stay long," she protested faintly, becoming increasingly aware of his fingers as they pressed ever so firmly against the lacy fabric of her sleeve. She swallowed hard and tried to think of something else to say as they crossed the brick-lined path that connected pasture and stables with the main house.

"Lucky for you it's not cold," he said, indicating her shoeless feet. "Still, I think we might just have something your size."

"That's really okay," she said, wondering why he was being so accommodating. She'd originally pegged him as a bored, rich playboy with too much money and time for his own or anyone else's good, and he wasn't that way at all.

When Kat was an impressionable teenager at St. Crispin's Academy for Girls, she'd longed to date one of the rich boys from Huntley Acres Prep, but as a Racanelli she wasn't quite up to snuff. Still, in her senior year she managed a real coup by snagging Byron Temple-Smythe as her date for the prom. His parents discovered that she was a scholarship student and the granddaughter of Italian immigrants who owned Rosa Motta's Ristorante, and they quickly put an end to the budding romance.

Kat's devastation at this subtle form of prejudice quickly turned to an if-you-can't-join-'em, lick-'em attitude that sent her to the top of her graduating class, and on to a full scholarship at the University of Virginia. Sensitive from this early snub, she'd devoted herself to her studies day and night, made honors and graduated Phi Beta Kappa. Kat's star shone brightly throughout veterinarian school, but undoubtedly the happiest day in her life was when she met fellow vet student, Jack Philips. Whatever angry memories she had of Byron Temple-Smythe evaporated that sunny afternoon when Jack took her for a ride on the back of his motorcycle. It was their first date, and it was the day she fell in love.

"Make yourself at home," Rafe was saying as they cleared the entranceway, "and I'll get us some coffee." He flicked a wall switch and recessed lighting bloomed in a sunken living room. His gaze traveled from Kat's crown of white carnations to her stocking feet. "Size four, five?"

"Four, but—"

"If the slipper fits..." Rafe murmured, as a smile touched his lips. He showed her the way to the living room, then he turned and made his way down the darkened hall.

Kat felt her cheeks burn, and was surprised at the unexpected pleasure this sensation caused. It was two o'clock in the morning. A couple of hours ago she had been toasting her youngest sister's happiness, and now she was standing on a cold tile floor in Rafe Sinclair's much-talked-about bachelor mansion. Wriggling her toes, she noticed holes in both stockings. Great! she thought. Just great. But as she stepped onto the cool marble stairs that flowed into the living room she decided that that was what came from dancing—and helping a mare give birth—without shoes.

Craning her neck, Kat let out an audible sigh as she gazed at the cathedral ceiling that arched above her. Dark beams crisscrossed against the cream-colored walls inlaid with gray stone; three oblong skylights revealing the night sky lent the room a spacious and open feeling. Kat automatically took a deep breath, as if she might draw in the cool, pine-scented night air; the aroma of leather, wood smoke and something decidedly masculine filled her nostrils. A shiver went through her, though the room was pleasantly warm.

Stepping onto the plush carpeting of the sunken living room added to the delicious sensations Kat was feeling. Padding slowly across the muted gray carpet was like getting a foot massage. Rafe had said to make herself at home, but oddly enough it was as if she *were* at home. Of course that could be because of the *Times Dispatch* article she'd read the other day: its full-page color spread had featured "Mr. Sinclair's" racehorse farm, River Run. The story pointed out that breeding racehorses was just a hobby; his real love and life's work was architecture.

Kat went into an adjoining library to find that Rafe had that uncanny sense of design—functional, yet as pleasing to the eye as a work of art. Aside from the glassed-in bookshelves and the bar, the library with its arched ceilings, skylights and stone fireplace was a smaller, cozier version of the living room.

Running her hand across the back of one of two chesterfield couches that flanked the hearth, Kat felt a sensation of pleasure creep up her arm. The material was a rich burgundy leather, and as she circled around the couch she gave in to the impulse to sink onto it. Tucking up her feet, she suddenly felt as if she'd been wrapped in a cocoon.

A sound from the living room drew her attention, and looking over her shoulder she saw Marty enter the library. He was carrying a silver tray that appeared to be loaded with a coffeepot, cups, saucers and a loaf of dark bread.

"Madam!" he said with a flourish in his English accent, then pushing aside several copies of *Architectural Digest,* set the tray onto the brass coffee table between the two couches. There was a mischievous twinkle in his eye as he added, "Shall I pour?"

"I'd be delighted," Kat said with a laugh. Then, leaning forward, she said, "You're butlering for your brother?"

Screwing his face to look like something he'd probably seen on late-night TV, he answered in a Cockney accent, "It's like this, me lady, when I'm in between wives I come and 'elp the chap out. One lump or two?"

"Black is fine."

Marty gave her a wink, then sitting on the couch beside her, handed the steaming cup of coffee to her. "You know, a shot of brandy would do wonders for it."

"Thanks, but this really is fine." Kat wrapped her hands around the cup, and silently regarded the man before her.

"Rafe is getting you some shoes," Marty said after a pause. Getting off the couch, he made his way to a bar across from the fireplace. It was an impressive piece: dark, scarred wood complete with a brass foot rail and a shiny spittoon. It reminded Kat of the old TV reruns of *Gunsmoke*. Marty's reflection was captured by a beveled-edge mirror that ran the length of the bar. He smiled up at her as he withdrew a bottle of brandy, then having topped his coffee with a shot of it, he ambled back and folded himself onto the couch opposite her.

"I really don't need the shoes." Kat withdrew her feet and with a shrug regarded them as if they were inanimate objects. "After all, it's just a short drive back to my place, and I do have other shoes."

"Not to worry," Marty assured her. After a swallow of coffee, he added, "You know you were really good at that foaling business. I don't know what would have happened if I hadn't suddenly decided to check on Nightstar. One thing's for sure though, Rafe would have been pretty upset if anything had happened to her."

"Don't you have a farm manager who keeps watch over a mare about to foal?"

"Oh yes, but he's down with that virus that's been going around, and since Nightstar's never foaled early before, none of us expected this. Rafe would never have gone to the Coast if he'd thought there might be a problem." Marty looked up and said, "Speak of the devil, or perhaps I should say Prince Charming, here he is, slipper in tow."

"As long as it's not made of glass!" Kat laughed. Twisting around, she felt her breath catch in her throat at the sight of Rafe. How could she have missed the sizzle in those movie-star blue eyes, or that thick blond hair swept back from that tanned and rugged face. Country club tan, not at all my type, she tried telling herself as he moved toward her. Gone was his pin-striped business suit. In its place was a pair of snug black jeans, black turtleneck sweater and cowboy boots. He looked as sleek as one of his racehorses, and she could tell from the look in his eyes that he was a person who was used to taking first place.

"I should probably kneel at your feet like they do in shoe stores," Rafe said with a laugh as he handed her a pair of sneakers. "As you can see, these don't even remotely resemble glass slippers, and I'm afraid they don't quite go with what you are wearing."

"They'll do just fine," she managed to say as she fumbled with the shoelaces.

"Here, let me do that." Rafe's hand closed over hers, and for a ridiculous moment their eyes locked over the pair of tennis shoes. Relinquishing them, Kat felt her cheeks flush as he joined her on the sofa, his arm jostling hers, causing a little jolt of electricity to pass through her. She was utterly tongue-tied. She tried to tell herself it was nonsense.

"Done!" Rafe exclaimed. He trailed one hand over the back of the couch and looked at her in a way that made her feel as if he were about to consume her on the spot.

"Thanks," she murmured in a voice she hardly recognized.

"Aren't you going to ask me where I got them?" he asked after a beat, his hand still draped over the couch.

"Oh...sure..." She threw him an appreciative look over her shoulder, then straightening up, managed a bit of humor. "You've got elves working in the basement, right?"

"How perceptive of you to notice." Rafe's smile flashed unexpectedly. "Actually, those tennies belong to my niece, but she'll be delighted to learn that our new horse vet wore them home."

"I'll return them tomorrow," Kat quickly put in.

"I'll hold you to it."

"But I'm really not your new horse vet—"

"Sure you are," Marty said as he crossed back to the bar. "I may not know a lot about horses, but I can spot a pro." He splashed some more brandy into his coffee mug, then hooking his heel on the rail, leaned against the bar. "If it hadn't been for you, there's no telling what would have happened to Nightstar. Right, Rafe?"

"Nightstar was just fine," Kat countered. "Besides, as I tried telling you over the phone—" she made a vague gesture in the air "—and again in the barn...I'm not an equine vet, I'm a—"

"You're *not* a vet?" Rafe sounded as if he might choke. There was a pause, then, "If you're not a vet, what the hell are you?"

"She's a vet," Marty interjected as he pushed away from the bar. "I looked her up in the phone book."

"Yes, yes. Of course I'm a vet. If you'd just let me explain—"

"Please do." As all warmth in Rafe's voice dropped, Kat felt as if the door to Antarctica had just blown open. She searched his blue eyes, but found them icy and impersonal.

She had a feeling this man had two speeds: fascination or aloofness, and Kat wasn't comfortable with either one. "Well?" he prodded.

"I'm a cat vet!" she blurted out, hastily rising to her feet. Then, for a single, unexpectedly gratifying moment, she realized she'd caught Rafe completely off guard. Kat started across what felt like miles of carpeting, then gaining the hall, she turned around and with a sense of delicious satisfaction, added, "I tend cats . . . and an occasional guinea pig."

Neither brother had moved. It was as if she had just issued a curse that had turned them to stone. With a lopsided smile, Kat wheeled around and headed out the door. She seriously doubted she'd be seeing much of the Sinclairs in the future. Somehow they didn't look the type to have cats *or* guinea pigs!

Chapter Two

"Just a minute!" Rafe's voice curled around Kat like a whip, stopping her in her tracks. "Do you have any idea of the complications that could have happened?" His easy, long-legged stride brought him alongside her, and she found herself looking up into fathomless blue eyes. "Nightstar is a horse, not some damn—"

"Racehorse, five years ago," Marty corrected from his position at the bar.

"I know that she's a horse," Kat managed airily.

"Yes. A horse, not some damn cat—"

"Do you have something against cats?" She felt the back of her neck bristle.

"You're missing the point," Rafe mumbled as he walked around her and headed for the hallway. "Delivering a premature foal isn't the same as delivering a litter of kittens!"

"I'm well aware of that, Mr. Sinclair," Kat rejoined, following him into the hall. "And since I *did* graduate from vet school I just might—"

"Specializing in *Garfield?*"

"Garfield?" she said indignantly. He wheeled around and she she nearly collided with him. The smell of leather and spicy after-shave assailed her. She was planted to the spot, all five feet of her staring up at what had to be all six feet of him. Faint light splashed against his high cheekbones and danced in his crystal eyes. There was something unpredictable about him that made Kat's well-schooled heart beat double-time. She wanted to say something snappy and clever, but her brain refused to cooperate; she also wanted to get as far away from the man as possible, but her legs had turned to jelly.

"You know, Garfield-the-cat. *Cats,* they're your specialty. You said so yourself, even your name supports it." The unexpected smile that hit his face disarmed her completely. "Never heard of a girl called Horse before. Horse-faced maybe, but that's not exactly a compliment. And certainly no one could ever call you *that.*" His approving gaze skimmed over her, then with a nod of his head he added, "So, what do you charge?"

Kat blinked in disbelief: the man turned his charm off and on like a faucet.

"Well?" His impersonal tone suggested she had just done something as mundane as cleaning his house. "Let me put it this way. If you *were* a vet—"

"I am a vet!" she snapped back with surprising vigor.

"If you were a large-animal vet," he smoothly corrected as he uncapped his pen, "how much would you charge for foaling at one-thirty in the morning?" Then, gesturing with the pen toward the turquoise lace, he said, "I'll gladly pay the dry-cleaning bill."

"You needn't bother," Kat replied testily. Of course, she could have told him that her deceased husband had been an equine vet and that more than once she'd helped him deliver foals. Kat knew only too well about the possible complications, but hell could freeze over before she'd tell Rafe Sinclair any of that.

"And as for my fee—"

"I trust this will cover it," Rafe said. After signing the check with that infuriating ease of the well-to-do, he crossed over to Kat and started to hand it to her.

"Thanks, but I wouldn't dream of taking your money under false pretenses."

"Don't be ridiculous."

"You thought I was an equine vet, and, and well, I just can't take your money!"

"Isn't it a little late for ethics?" There was an amused glint in his eye as he playfully waved the check in front of her nose.

"Ethics?" Kat shot the word back to him like a ball in a Ping-Pong game.

"Yes, you know, medical ethics? Don't you take some sort of oath like doctors do?" His mouth curved in a delicious smile. "Hey, just take the check." He tucked it in her hand, but she thrust it back.

"Make it out to the S.P.C.A.!" Once again she found herself craning her neck to look up him. Was that amusement in his eyes? She didn't want to stick around to find out. She muttered a time-honored Italian curse she'd so often heard her nana use, and wheeling about she resolutely headed once again for the door.

"Hey, you know, I should be the one on a tear, not you," Rafe said, dogging her footsteps.

"Listen, it's been a long day, so let's just call a truce."

"I fly off the handle sometimes," Rafe explained with disarming abruptness, then placing his hands on her shoulders, he slowly turned her to face him. "My aunt says I'm an unpredictable Aquarian." The pressure of his fingers sent lightning down her arms, and he was smiling that smile again—the one Kat found as potent as a shot of sodium Pentothal. It immobilized her, made her practically forget her name. But then he was an Aquarian, she reminded herself. According to Nana Aquarians had electric magnetism that put them light-years ahead of their peers. As far as Kat was concerned, he could stay there. Another galaxy suited him just fine.

"Aquarians, I believe, are also called the eccentrics of the zodiac, so nothing you do would really surprise me." She took a steadying breath, and added, "At any rate, I *do* understand your concern for Nightstar, and naturally I'll check back on her and the foal. You were lucky we didn't have to send them into the clinic for monitoring." Reaching into her purse, Kat withdrew her card. "In any case, feel free to call if you need to reach me." Putting her business card on the table by the door, she turned and made as smooth an exit as possible. From the corner of her eye she spotted Marty, pipe in one hand and coffee cup in the other, leaning indolently against the arched doorway leading to the living room.

The temperature outside had dropped considerably, but Kat received the slap of cold air as a welcome friend come to sober her up. The fog had completely lifted, and the moon, like a burnished penny, rolled slowly toward the horizon, leaving the sky a pale indigo with a smattering of stars in its wake.

River Run Farm wasn't that far from her cottage, but the late hour and the winding country roads made the drive home seem longer. Nevertheless, Kat felt she could use the time to sort out her thoughts. According to her grandmother, that wasn't *all* she needed. Nana felt she needed a good man and plenty of TLC. Of course, Kat had told her countless times that it was a lot of nonsense, but the pain beneath her carefree facade made a liar of her. Long hours at work hadn't helped, either, and even though it was a year and a half since Jack's death, she still didn't feel safe enough to even consider another man.

However, Rafe Sinclair was not just *another man,* and the sudden, raw emotions he uprooted left Kat feeling vulnerable and in need of love. Love was something she'd thought she buried along with Jack Philips. How could she love anyone after Jack?

As she turned off Blacksmith Lane onto Kennebeck Road, memories of Jack flashed by like a speeded-up film— the tall, dark and handsome football hero whom as an undergrad she'd never had the nerve to meet; the crazy guy who broke his arm falling out of a tree trying to get a cat. Then came vet school and that sunny afternoon when a friend had introduced them. With an infectious friendliness, Jack had offered her a ride on his Harley. He'd kissed her that afternoon, too. It was her first real kiss, and she was certain the earth had moved. Someone actually *loved* little Katrina Racanelli. She knew it was love, and had wanted to shout it from the rooftops.

Slowing down for the turn into her driveway, Kat shook the past from her thoughts. There wasn't really any point in dwelling on memories, even if most of them were happy. The unhappy memory was the one she couldn't quite remember: the stable fire.

Bringing the truck to a halt, she bit down on her lower lip as sadness suddenly enfolded her. Jack's death should never have happened, *wouldn't* have happened if only... if only she had... done what? The doctors had told her that eventually she would remember everything, and then she could bury her grief. They had even suggested hypnotism to speed the process along. Kat had tried it; it didn't work. Neither did the antidepressants they prescribed. Kat knew she was lucky to have survived the fire, lucky to have had the finest plastic surgeon available, but although the doctor removed the facial scars, he was unable to reach the scars beneath the surface.

Kat had wanted to die, and if it hadn't been for her family urging her to return home to Pineboro, she might have.

Surrounded by whispers of the past, Kat sat a moment longer in Jack's old red pickup truck. He'd wanted leather seats, and had liked the fact that the scent reminded Kat of her grandfather's antique Packard. Memories piled on memories, thick as a scrapbook of fading photos. Put them away. Live in the present, she silently counseled herself as she got out of the truck.

She paused midway on the flagstone path that led to her cottage and breathed deeply of the crisp air. The moon had sunk behind a distant ridge of pines, leaving the sky studded with stars as bright as diamonds. Kat's mood slowly brightened, but then coming home to the cottage her grandfather had left her always brought a smile to her lips. Just down the road from the big house where Nana lived, this mid-eighteenth-century relic, nestled amid towering pines and old magnolias, was like a silent witness to the past.

More memories, she thought as she ducked beneath a low branch and cut across the remaining flagstones that led to the adjacent veterinary clinic. The sensor lights she'd just installed bloomed to life, illuminating her shingle, The Racanelli Veterinary Clinic. Kat hadn't been able to hang the one Jack had made for her, the one that read The Kat's Meow, Katrina R. Philips, D.V.M., with a small black cat curled up beside her name. That was all in her past, and best left undisturbed.

"I hear you, Killer," she murmured on entering the reception area, then bending over, she picked up the golden shaded Persian who'd wound himself around her ankles. Immense emerald eyes blinked back at her. After a plaintive meow, he plastered his owllike face against her neck and began to purr. Killer had been dropped off by a rich socialite with instructions to "gas the little monster." Apparently the cat had ruined her mink coat by spraying it!

Kat had refused to put him to sleep, saying that since she didn't have any animal coats she doubted there would be a problem. The Persian's name was Prince Ivan, but Kat's nephews had dubbed him Killer in the hopes that he'd catch mice. He didn't. He was afraid of them, but loved his new mistress *and* being top cat at the clinic.

In the evenings Killer always followed Kat through the corridor that led from her office to her cottage. Although he was a chatty little fellow who enjoyed extensive conversations with her, he was also quite content simply to be near her.

"Sorry I'm so late," she said, tucking the cat under her arm as she entered the small yet pristine kennel area, which held a dozen cages. Four cages were occupied by mewing feline boarders, one held a female tabby who'd just been spayed. After checking her patients, Kat and Killer made cursory rounds of the surgery and examining rooms. Although Kat didn't like to admit it, ever since the stable accident she'd had an unconscious fear of fire. She'd opened her clinic three months ago, and the first thing she'd done was to have smoke alarms and fire extinguishers put in every room. Despite the fact that the rooms were mostly tile and sparkling stainless steel, the building's wooden framework, dating from the 1770s, was definitely flammable.

"Well, Killer, it's three o'clock in the morning and past both of our bedtimes," Kat said on a yawn as she flicked out the lights and made her way back to her cottage.

She'd turned the passageway into a comic strip gallery featuring favorite felines: every cat from Sylvester to Garfield. Wouldn't Mr. Sinclair just love it!

"Some nerve that man has," she muttered to Killer, who was trotting toward his favorite room, the kitchen. "You would have thought I'd slipped his horse some strychnine, but then you know how some of these horse people are. I probably shouldn't have laid a finger on the mare, but considering the situation, what else could I do?" Kat entered the country-style kitchen and, retrieving a handful of kitty treats, rewarded Killer. Then, after pouring herself a glass of mineral water, she flipped out the light and started for the stairs. Tomorrow morning was going to come much too early. Even though her receptionist usually opened up at eight o'clock, patients frequently arrived earlier.

After slipping out of her bridesmaid's attire, Kat sank onto the edge of her bed and contemplated the two-tone tennis shoes. She didn't know many people who wore size four, but then maybe Rafe's niece was just a kid. Undoing the laces and yanking off the shoes, Kat realized with some chagrin that they had to be returned. She'd do it during lunch hour tomorrow, and hopefully avoid Rafe.

Basta! Enough! Kat muttered as she finished washing her face. Rafe Sinclair was just a man. Repeating this sentiment to the mirror, she stared at what she considered to be an unremarkable face: although the pale olive complexion was smooth, its shape was hopelessly round; the mouth was too large and the nose too small. Brandy-colored eyes, however, combined with her cap of cropped, glossy black hair to give her an elfish look that Jack had always found appealing.

Flicking out the light, Kat dashed across the icy hallway to her bedroom. Killer screeched past his mistress and catapulted onto the center of the massive four-poster that dominated the small Colonial-style room. Lost in the mound of fluffy pink comforter, only the swish of his golden tail could be seen.

With a laugh, Kat ruffled his fur. Getting into bed, she adjusted the pillows, drew the comforter around her and reached for the mystery novel she was halfway through.

It was strange how a little murder before bed could chase back the shadows. Ever since she discovered the power of "whodunits" two weeks ago, the terrible nightmares about the fire had almost stopped. Maybe, just maybe, life was headed back to normal. After all, she'd managed to go back to practicing veterinary medicine again. Surely that was a step in the right direction, especially considering how she'd felt after Jack's death.

"Basta," she repeated softly, then opening the book, lost herself to mayhem.

"There are night people, and there are day people," Marty said as he spread out a hand of solitaire, "and since it's three in the morning, that makes me a day person. Or maybe I should say *morning* person." Raising his coffee cup, he met the inquisitive glance of his brother. "And you needn't fear I'm going to drink myself to death over this last divorce. Like an actor I am merely in-between engagements, and alas, I fear making up for your bachelorhood." He slapped down several cards. "This is pure coffee—black enough to hold up my spoon. You look like you could use a cup. Might help with whatever the hell you're doodling on."

"Lot number twenty-eight in the Pendleton Acres development," Rafe replied wearily as he leaned against his drawing board and ran long fingers through his hair.

"Does my presence deter the muse?"

"The muse has gone to sleep, and I'm about to follow." Rafe smiled at his older half brother; although ten years and a continent had divided them most of their lives, they had grown close in the past two years.

"That was *some* vet," Marty remarked as he scanned the cards before him. "Although I suppose apologies are in order since I dragged the wrong kind to your stable." He slapped down another card, then allowed a slow smile to curve his lips. "The wrong kind of vet, that is."

"She did her job," Rafe said, rocking back in his chair. "Actually, I'm surprised she knew as much as she did about horses."

"I'll lay you odds that dark-haired filly knows quite a bit about all sorts of animals . . . if you catch my meaning."

"You're the expert on the opposite sex," Rafe acknowledged, resuming his work.

Looking up from his cards, Marty said, "Just had more practice, old chap. However, let's get back to you, because as odd as it might sound, I'm here to help you find a wife."

"To find a *what?*" Rafe turned on his stool to face his brother. "In the week that you've been here, you've decided to appoint yourself my personal Cupid?"

"I've been mulling it over for some time, and believe me, if anyone knows about picking a mate, it's got to be me."

"Right," Rafe said as he swiveled back to his drawing board. "Maybe you should write a book on it—probably make the bestseller list." He tried to sound flip, in the hope that Marty would drop the subject.

He didn't.

"Dad wrote me several months ago, after you and Millicent had broken off, said he was worried about you, that you'd been dating a steady stream of—"

"Bimbos?" Rafe supplied, nodding his head. "That's what Aunt Mimi calls them, too. But it's not cause for a family council." He pushed away from his drawing board once again, then rose and crossed to the massive arched window that overlooked his property. Thrusting his hands into his jeans pockets, he stared at a distant ridge of pines, their lacy pattern highlighted by a pale disk of moon as it slipped closer to the horizon. And then there was the James River, barely visible, which moved like a thin, silvery snake on those distant mossy banks. The river that in his youth had so captured his imagination. As a child, living at Kennebeck Plantation, he'd planned his whole life around that river. In school he had been taught that civilizations practically rose and fell on the banks of mighty rivers. That was when Rafe decided he would become an architect, and design a home right next to the one his family had owned since before the Civil War. He'd call it River Run, and he'd marry and have children to leave it to.

However, some dreams turn to ashes before the foundation is even built. It was one thing to forge a successful career, especially given the silver spoon Rafe knew he'd been born with. But how to find and marry that special person? That was another story altogether.

Shaking off these thoughts, he slowly turned and started for his studio door.

"Let's talk about the bimbos." Marty's voice suggested they might be discussing the stock market.

"An empty topic," Rafe replied on a yawn.

"Righto! Then we can move on to Dr. Racanelli."

"*You* can move on to her, I'll opt for a bypass."

"You make it sound like surgery," Marty said, slapping down his last card. "Anyway, I'm really not in the market. Not yet, that is."

Rafe paused by the door. "Listen, big brother, Dr. R. and I get along about as well as a fox and a hound in a training pen."

"Tsk, tsk. Such imagery." Shuffling his cards, Marty asked, "Are you the hound or the fox?"

"Oh, for Pete's sake, it was a figure of speech."

"And an incorrect one, because—unless I need stronger glasses—until you found out she was a cat doctor there *were* a few sparks in the air. Granted, not enough for a forest fire, but a nice, contained blaze on the hearth—"

"You've got an overactive imagination," Rafe muttered, starting for the door once more.

"You were kneeling at her feet talking about glass slippers, as I recall." Marty slanted a look at his brother, then turned back to his new game of solitaire.

"Put your bow away. You're way off target."

"Am I?"

"You are!" Rafe took a deep breath; he needed his brother's interference about as much as two left arms. "I'm going to check on Nightstar and the foal, then turn in."

"Dr. R. said she'd be by tomorrow," Marty reminded him with a wink.

"Great. Since you're the one who called her in the first place, I'm sure you'll be able to handle her."

"I'll give her your regards," his brother called after him, then turning over the ace of hearts, sent it sailing in Rafe's direction. "It's not going to be solitaire for you much longer, old chap."

"Leave the soothsaying to Aunt Mimi." Rafe flipped the card back to Marty and headed out the door.

Chapter Three

Kat wrinkled up her nose in delight as she sampled the eggplant Parmesan. She turned to her older sister, Tonia, and said, "This is the best yet. The customers are really in for a treat!" She plopped her spoon in the industrial dishwasher, then with pot holder in hand, turned her attention to an enormous iron caldron of bubbling minestrone. Lifting the lid, she gave an approving sniff.

"But as for forgetting to leave off the tennis shoes," Kat said, picking up the thread of their earlier conversation, "there was no hidden meaning behind it."

"Whatever you say, Sis," Tonia replied, disappearing into the walk-in refrigerator.

"Please, no amateur psychology!" Kat said on a laugh as she snagged a piece of steaming garlic bread. Easing herself onto a nearby stool, she took a thoughtful bite out of it. "The important thing is that the foal and mother are doing fine, and I managed to avoid the owner. Hey, Earth to Tonia! Can you hear me?"

"I'm in the walk-in, I'll be back in a second," Tonia replied in a muffled voice.

The Racanellis had recently remodeled the restaurant's kitchen, adding a private alcove where the chef could prepare special dishes in relative quiet. Just beyond that lay the walk-in fridge, the main kitchen and chaos; the din of voices, clanging of silverware and china and the interminable rumble of a dishwasher was about as deafening as a rock concert. As much as Katrina enjoyed cooking, she had always known that working at the family restaurant would have been for her a nightmare. Luckily for her parents, Kat's brothers and sisters seemed to thrive at Rosa Motta's. Despite Kat's aversion to the heat of the kitchen, she loved the food, and whenever time allowed would pop in for lunch or dinner.

"By the way," Kat called out, "this garlic bread is heavenly, although it will probably drive away all my patients."

"Vampires beware!" Tonia declared, as she finally reappeared, loaded down with a sack of carrots. She hurled it onto the stainless steel counter, then began pulling the carrots out of their burlap bag.

Dear Tonia, Kat's much adored older sister: the tall, auburn-haired beauty of the family who, at thirty-two, still preferred sharing head-chef duties with their older brother, Gustavo, to getting married and settling down.

"So what's wrong with the horse owner?" Tonia asked, looking up from her work.

"Everything!" Kat leveled a serious look at her sister. "You, having turned down three marriage proposals, are asking me a question like that?"

"They were all poor risks and, according to Nana, my Cancer planets make me a security nut. Although they also make me a good cook, and oh, so modest!" Tonia murmured as her knife sliced carrots with the lightning speed of a cuisine machine.

"Nana says a lot of things."

"Don't tell me…the tone of your voice sounds like you're meeting her for lunch, and I'll bet she's—"

"She'd better not! If it's like last time, I don't know what I'll do."

"I'll bet she's got you another one of those blind dates from Date a Star Mate!"

"Right. Like the triple Virgo C.P.A. Nana had mixed up with the Aquarian veterinarian. Or how about the Scorpio millionaire heart surgeon?"

"Oh, yeah, the one whose idea of a *discreet* relationship meant not letting his wife know." With a wink, Tonia gave her sister a sprig of parsley. "Nevertheless, you might want to chew on that in case Nana *does* bring Mr. Right, 'cause there's a ton of garlic on that bread."

"In that case, I'll have another piece," Kat replied wickedly. "Besides, maybe, just maybe Nana will be alone."

"Then why didn't she just pop in your cottage, or have you up to her house? I know, I know," she said, throwing up her hands, "she's got this sentimental attachment to the restaurant."

"Yes, and since it's Tuesday she'll probably order Alfredo Romano," Kat said, jumping off the stool.

"Hey, this might just be an innocent lunch. With Mom and Pop vacationing in Fort Lauderdale, Nana probably imagines the restaurant going down the tubes. Undoubtedly makes her feel better to be around the place." Tonia gave her sister a grin and a thumbs-up.

Mirroring the gesture, Kat said, "You're probably right. After all, she and Nonno started the business."

"Sit at table three so Elena can wait on you. That way, if Nana brings another star-date, Sis can dump a little minestrone in his lap."

Kat turned around. "*If* an Astro-Mate does appear, I'll suddenly remember a very sick cat who's in need of an injection."

Much to Katrina's relief, Nana appeared solo, although from the devilish look on her grandmother's face, Kat half expected The Man to pop out from behind her grandmother's plum-colored caftan.

"Such a face you have on, *bambina mia,*" Rosa said as she embraced her granddaughter. Then, entwining her pudgy arm through Kat's slender one, she led them past the throng of noon customers to their table. Although the restaurant was packed with people, carpeted floors and high ceilings kept the noise to a minimum, and unlike many restaurants, Rosa Motta's allowed a generous spacing between tables, many of which overlooked an outdoor garden café.

They sat at one of those tables, and as Rosa sank into her chair she let out a sigh. Indicating the garden's centerpiece, a Roman fountain, she murmured, "Ah, when spring comes and the gods are once more spouting the water, can you think of a better place for a wedding? *Sì?*"

"Some people might say a church," Kat replied with a grin as she opened the menu out of habit.

"*Spero che sì!* But I mean for the reception." With a sweep of her hand, she gestured toward the Italian street scenes that papered the walls. "You know the old saying, *Vedi Napoli e poi mori.*"

"Yes, Nana—see Naples and die." Kat was only too familiar with the various Italian sayings and fables, and probably someday she, too, would repeat them to her grandchildren. But when she looked up from the menu, the sight of Rafe Sinclair entering the restaurant wiped out that thought completely. Abruptly she hid behind the menu, but not before his eyes met hers. Cautiously, Kat peered over the rim of the menu as Rafe and his companion, a curvaceous blonde, were being led in the opposite direction. Although relieved by this near miss, Kat also felt oddly let down. Pushing this thought aside, however, she quickly turned her attention back to her grandmother.

"So you see," Rosa concluded cheerfully, "one can come to our restaurant and see *our* Napoli, and save so much money. Then someday they can die in peace." Gazing at the mural depicting a flaming sunset over Capri, she let out another sigh. "Still, I tell you, Rosa Motta's would be perfect for the reception. We have everything here—even the grand banquet hall upstairs with room for an orchestra. Very formal, very proper," she murmured, tapping the menu with her plump little fingers. "Or, if we choose the patio, we could have a band."

"Whoa, Nana," Kat said, reaching across the checked tablecloth and patting her grandmother's hands. "We just had a wedding yesterday! Maria's, remember? Besides, who's this *we* you keep referring to?"

Ignoring the question, Rosa merely shrugged her shoulders. "You should always be prepared, because you never know when that special someone is going to pop into your life."

"Lucky for me I have a restaurant for just such an emergency." Narrowing her eyes, Kat asked, "You sure you don't have something hidden up your sleeves?"

"*Dio mio!* Such a suspicious nature!"

"Well, can you blame me after those last star-souls you tried to hitch me to?"

"I admit it was a bit hasty on my part. But today's lunch is very different. I have news from Mrs. Chandler." Rosa smiled and several gold teeth gleamed, then pursing her lips solemnly together, she added, "Still, my astrology helped your sister Maria with Greg."

"Yes, but you didn't exactly pluck him out of the Date a Star Mate catalog. In fact, come to think of it, you didn't introduce them at all."

"I picked their wedding date, and that counts a great deal. If I had left it up to your mother, there's no telling what would have happened! And to think my own daughter gave me such a hard time because it was at eleven o'clock on Monday night. Still, we had a pretty good party afterward, didn't we?"

"The best, Nana!" Kat admitted with a laugh.

"However, if Maria had waited until spring, there were several Saturdays with good aspects, *and* the reception could have been on the patio. Imagine how divine it would have been with the Bernini Fountain going. By the way, what sort of cat emergency called you away last night anyway?"

"It's a long story," Kat replied, glancing at her menu once again. What would Rafe have thought if he knew about the Monday night wedding? Chances were she'd never find out; although she was certain if he knew the reason was astrology, he'd label it as a bunch of hocus-pocus. She didn't really want to think of the label he'd stuck on *her*. Undoubtedly if she saw much of him, she'd probably find out, but then Kat had no intention of that happening. If only she'd remembered to return the tennis shoes this morning when she'd checked on Nightstar. As it stood now, she'd be doing well to eat lunch and make an exit before Rafe and his luncheon date reappeared.

Closing her menu as if closing the book on Rafe Sinclair, Kat said, "I'm with you—let's both have the Alfredo Romano." Then, looking up expectantly at her grandmother, she added, "So, what's this about Mrs. Chandler?"

"Ah, a wonderful opportunity for you, my dear," Rosa murmured, as she signaled for her other granddaughter, Elena, to come and get their order. "Oh, but I am so lucky to be surrounded by my family!"

Kat winked up at her younger sister, who stood poised with pencil and pad. "Nana and I'll have the same—Alfredo Romano, a salad with the house dressing, two hot teas and something gooey for dessert!"

"Of course, dessert!" Nana confirmed with a grin. "Nice big ones."

As Elena headed for the kitchen, Rosa leaned forward and said, "Now, I know you've never really been interested in working at the restaurant, and that's all right, what with Gustavo and Tonia in the kitchen and little Elena out here and Maria as bookkeeper, but still sometimes I think there should be some place for my Katrina—"

"You haven't forgotten that I'm a vet, have you?" Kat bit down on a sudden bubble of laughter, wondering just what her grandmother was planning this time.

"*Dio mio,* of course not! Although you still make the best lasagna verde in the whole family. Still, this is not about you working in the restaurant. After all, what would happen to the poor cats?"

"And you don't have a star-mate waiting for me in the lobby?" Kat teased as her sister slid their salads and garlic bread before them.

"I learned my lesson about that!" Rosa said, waving her fork in the air. Then, plunging it into a juicy tomato, she added, "My good friend Mrs. Chandler is giving a surprise birthday party for her young nephew this Friday and the restaurant is catering it." She paused for a bite of salad, her dark eyes all the while fastened intently on Katrina.

"That's nice," Kat said, waiting for the inevitable other shoe to fall. "I suppose Gus will be pretty busy making up all those ice-cream figurines. How many kids are going to be there?''

"Oh, I'm not sure.'' Rosa's gaze fell to her salad, then looking up at Kat, she quickly said, "But that won't be your department, anyway.''

"Aha! So *I* am involved in this little effort!'' Triumphantly she speared a cucumber and brandished it in mid-air.

"Well, normally I don't have much say on these things anymore, but since Mrs. Chandler is my friend...''

"Yes?''

"Of course, Maria normally handles the hostess end, but since she's on her honeymoon...''

"You'd like me to do it?''

"Would you?''

"Sure,'' Kat replied with a laugh. "All you had to do was ask. It's not like I'm booked up Friday and Saturday nights.''

"Such a pity! Ah, but it is good this Friday you are free.''

"I take it we're going to help with the decorations?''

"It's going to be fairly simple,'' Rosa replied.

"Will the party have a theme?''

Rosa's eyes twinkled mischievously. "Well, since it's Valentine's Day, I suppose that could be the theme.''

"Hearts and flowers translates to spin the bottle and post office?''

"Like I say, you don't have to worry about that end of it, you just show up and help Mrs. Chandler. Gus and his crew will handle the food, and the...guests...can handle the games. Though of course you will dress accordingly. You might want to wear your red silk—you know, the one with the rhinestones on the jacket.''

"To a birthday party?" At Nana's nod, Kat pictured the scarlet cocktail dress with its spaghetti straps and matching jacket.

"You'll be the hostess. It will be perfect."

Despite Kat's misgivings, she finally convinced herself that surely her grandmother, if a bit eccentric, was on the up-and-up this time. After all, what could possibly happen at a children's party? Besides, Nana wasn't even involved with it. Kat would be getting in touch with Mrs. Chandler the afternoon before the party. Chiding herself for being leery of her grandmother's motives, Kat dismissed her suspicions.

By the time she had scraped the last vestiges of the delectably creamy Alfredo Romano from her plate, Kat, feeling contentedly full and slightly sleepy, headed toward the coffee island for a refill. The usual noontime crowd was milling around the self-serve station, and after Kat had filled her cup to the brim, she started to squeeze through, only to be jostled by someone behind her. As the scalding coffee spilled onto her hand, she let out a cry and dropped the cup. Bending to pick up the broken pieces, she came eye to eye with none other than Rafe Sinclair.

"Ah, Dr. Racanelli!"

"Oh, I'm...I'm so sorry...." Leaning forward, Kat made an ineffectual swipe with her napkin at the coffee stain on the lapel of his charcoal-gray suit. Suddenly she felt his hand on hers.

"We've got to stop meeting like this." Was that humor she heard in his voice? Her heart was pounding so loudly she couldn't tell. His eyes, a dark blue, seemed almost black, and they were studying her intently. Then he rose gracefully, bringing her and the broken cup with him.

"Someone bumped into me from behind...I'm so sorry...."

"You're repeating yourself," he said, discarding the broken cup. "It was a chain reaction. Couldn't be helped. Can I get you another coffee?"

"No...I...that is, I think I'm sufficiently awake now." She didn't add that bumping into him had thrown her into overdrive.

"Marty said he caught a glimpse of your red truck as you were leaving this morning. You could have stopped in, you know." Stepping over to the coffee machine, he casually poured himself a cup.

"I didn't want to bother anyone. It was rather early."

"Marty would have enjoyed your company. Besides, it wasn't that early." He stirred his black coffee, then taking a sip, smiled at her above the rim of the cup. Damn Marty for his predictions! Yet here he was completely taken by this slip of a girl. However, from the way she was looking at him, you would have thought he'd just escaped from the nearest state prison. This wasn't the usual reaction Rafe got from women. But then he was beginning to suspect that Katrina Racanelli was in a class all her own.

"I believe your friend is waiting for you," she said with what sounded to him like a touch of self-satisfaction. Then, flashing him a wide smile, Kat added, "And I have an operation scheduled this afternoon. So..."

"So perhaps I'll drop by afterward for those sneakers," Rafe said softly. There was a surprised look in her eyes as if he'd announced he was going to kidnap her in a hot-air balloon. For that single moment she seemed young, naive and innocent. This was quickly replaced by a cool look.

"If I'm not there, either my receptionist or assistant will have them for you." She smiled, but it didn't quite reach her eyes. "I've really got to go now, and it looks like your friend is getting a bit impatient."

Twisting around, Rafe could see that Eleanor Forbes, re-linquishing her usual sultry moves, was bearing down on them. It seemed for a moment as if she and an older woman, looking vaguely like a gypsy fortune-teller, might collide.

Setting down his coffee cup, Rafe murmured a swift goodbye and, linking arms with Eleanor, smoothly led her toward the coatrack.

For some unaccountable reason he'd wanted to explain to Kat that Ms. Forbes was a client, the soon-to-be proud owner of lot twenty-eight in the Pendleton Acres develop-ment, and had no claim whatsoever on him. That he and the voluptuous, wealthy socialite had been seeing quite a bit of each other was beside the point. Hell, why did he care *what* Dr. Katrina Racanelli thought? Despite what Marty had said last night, she wasn't his type. His type was . . . was . . . well, more like Eleanor, he supposed.

As he helped Eleanor into her fur coat his glance strayed back to Kat. She met his eyes with an unblinking stare, then abruptly turned to the gypsy woman beside her. Well—let her keep the tennis shoes, he thought with a savageness that completely took him off guard.

"We'd better head over to the site before the rain comes," he heard himself saying. As Rafe met Eleanor's smile he wondered if he even knew *what* his type was. It had always been the chic, tall, blond sophisticates: full-lipped beauties who were properly coordinated on the outside, but resem-bled *Playboy* centerfolds underneath. Then there was Kat: short, raven-haired and . . . His eyes sought her out again, and were rewarded with a glimpse of heavy knit sweater and short skirt nicely accentuating her curves. She wasn't something for the country club, but then Rafe somehow doubted that she was a member. He smiled to himself as he watched her and her eccentric-looking companion thread their way to the door.

"Rafe?" The smooth, slightly high-pitched voice of his companion brought him out of his reverie. Looking at Eleanor's broad smile and row of perfect white teeth, he was reminded of magazine covers. Glossy, glazed and perfect— on the surface. He thought of the fire in Kat's dark eyes, of the small chip in her front tooth and of her lopsided smile.

Damn, he thought, he was going to have to retrieve those tennis shoes, after all. As Eleanor's arm pressed against him, a wave of thick perfume clouded the air, and he remembered something elusive and springlike about Kat. Lily of the valley in February?

"*Cara mia!* I so wanted to meet the tall stranger!" Rosa drew a slight pout as she snapped her seat belt in place. "He had the look of an Aquarian, and you know that a Leo and an Aquarian is a match made in heaven."

"You said that about the Scorpio heart surgeon," Kat gently reminded her as she exited onto Patterson Avenue. How on earth had Nana figured out his sign? She'd barely seen him!

"Aquarius is better. And that man had the look in his eye. Always you can tell by that look."

"Crazed?"

"No, no, no! These Aquarians are unique and eccentric. I cannot think how to say it! *Ma, dica me, dove—*"

"English, *per favore*. You know how bad my Italian is." Braking for a red light, Kat gave her grandmother a pat on the arm.

"Where did you meet this handsome Aquarian?" Rosa asked in a slow, measured voice.

"Nana, handsome Aquarian or not, he's definitely not my type. Besides, I doubt if we'll be seeing much of each other anyway. You saw the woman he was with."

"Aha! So you noticed her, too!"

"It was rather hard not to," Kat responded, tapping her fingers impatiently against the steering wheel. *Why wouldn't the darn light change?*

"Brassy!"

"What?"

"That overstuffed blonde was a brassy bimbo." Rosa threw Kat a self-congratulatory look. "This is a new word I learn from Mrs. Chandler."

"Brassy?" Kat accelerated as the light changed to green.

"No. Bimbo. English is such a wonderful language. I've been here many years, and always learning new expressions. Brassy blonde bimbo."

"She might be very nice," Kat protested, suddenly playing devil's advocate.

"They say Lucrezia Borgia was very nice—"

"Oh, Nana!"

"To her pet Pekinese," Rosa finished triumphantly. "I read it in *The American Intruder.*"

"Good Lord, that rag prints anything! Anyway, it has nothing to do with...with Rafe's friend." Despite the careless air with which she tossed off his name, Kat felt a twinge of green-eyed monster. Felt it and tried to squelch it—unsuccessfully. She'd even dreamed about the man last night, and from the remembered fragments she had a feeling that dream had a PG rating.

"Ah, now we're getting somewhere," Rosa said after a beat. "Rafe..."

"I don't know what sign he is, nor do I care. And please, Nana, don't start telling me how much I need a good man." Increasing their speed to fifty-five as they entered Pineboro County, Kat added, "I'm very happy, really, I am. Business is going very well, my new assistant is super, and if I clear enough money this spring I might even renovate the attic into a guest room."

"With your Virgo rising, business will always be good for you. The books will balance, but maybe not the heart."

"My heart's great. I jog, eat oatmeal for breakfast and have given up red meat." Kat tossed Rosa a smile, then softly added, "Give me time, Nana. I know it's been more than a year since Jack died, but I'm just not ready to go beating the bushes for another man. You know, Jack was pretty special."

Her throat tightened and she fell silent. If she tried to say so much as another word, tears would start rolling down her cheeks. From grief or guilt? Like knotted threads they had wound themselves so tightly around that heart of hers, she wasn't sure where one started and the other stopped.

"Mimi, did I not tell you that my Katrina and your Rafe would meet with a bang?" Rosa gripped the telephone receiver with one hand and coiled the cord around her other, then slowly sank onto the nearest chair.

"When?" her friend asked after a moment.

"I am not sure, but does he have cats?"

"Cats? You know, oddly enough I don't think he does. Although, come to think of it, most people in the country do." There was a slight pause, then, "Oh, that's right, Katrina is a veterinarian, and you think they met through her practice."

"It's the *only* way!"

"Well, let's see," Mimi drawled, "he has Mutt and Jeff— they're two dogs that had been dumped by the side of the road, and Rafe, with that big Aquarian heart of his, naturally took them in. Then there's Cuthbert, he's a fifteen-year-old Great Dane—he might have taken sick. Are you sure this man she met was my Rafe?"

"Like you described him—very tall with the light hair and such blue eyes, even from a distance I could see them. Besides, she used his name."

"Oh, then you didn't actually meet him?"

"No, but even before I got his name out of Kat, I told her he was an Aquarian because of the look about the eyes. Ah, but do not worry, Mimi, my granddaughter suspects nothing."

"So she'll be there Friday night for the birthday party?"

"In a red silk dress! She will look so beautiful. Ah, but already I could see the sparks between them." Rosa tendered a sigh, leaving off the fact that they were sparks of war and not grand passion. "Well, why are you so silent? Do you mind the red silk?"

"Oh, no. Red is one of Rafe's favorite colors. It's just that I seem to remember something about Rafe being allergic to cats when he was a child."

"Oh, *dio mio! È impossibile!*" Cradling the receiver between her ample chins and shoulder, Rosa reached into her candy dish for a chocolate caramel. Surely Mimi had to be mistaken.

On a characteristic outflow of breath, Kat ruffled her bangs, stripped off and disposed of her surgical gloves and pushed her way through the operating-room doors, headed for the watercooler to quench her thirst. Then she'd go back in and help Annie, her assistant, finish cleaning up.

The operation had been a little more complicated than either of them had anticipated. The old tomcat's infection had turned out to be a nasty abcess that went deep into the jawbone, requiring extensive cleaning. If the owners had waited much longer, it was doubtful he'd have pulled through. As it was, he'd needed a blood transfusion and extensive antibiotic therapy.

Still, operations like this one called on all of Kat's reserves. Because she was doing something that made a difference, it brought out the best in her. Surgery kept her busy, too, and when she was busy she couldn't think about Jack, or for that matter, Rafe.

Rafe. Of all the places in Richmond, why did he have to turn up at Rosa Motta's? Unbidden, his face rose up before her. Handsome, angular and taunting. She could see the dancing light in his eyes as they met hers—eyes that seemed to look right through her.

Nana would say meeting him was destiny. Was it fate that made her drop her coffee cup? And was it the spilled coffee that had burned her, or the touch of his hands? The hands of an architect: big, capable hands with long fingers and square, neat nails. Nana always said you could tell a lot about a man by the shape of his hands.

As Kat leaned against the watercooler and slowly drank her water, she wondered what it would feel like to have those same hands slip through her hair, then slowly drift down her neck, all the while pulling her toward him; toward the bright lights in his eyes, toward lips that looked as if they knew how to kiss a woman....

An abrupt knock at the door jolted her back to reality. What on earth had come over her? Knowing full well where her daydream was headed, Kat felt flaming color splash against her cheeks. What kind of power did this Rafe Sinclair have over her anyway? She hadn't even thought about a man *that way* since Jack died. Couldn't allow herself to. Not yet. No, and not for a long time, she told herself.

"I've got it, Annie," she called out, as she crossed to the door and opened it. "You!"

"Is that how you always greet your clients?" Rafe cocked his head and studied her. He knew his scrutiny annoyed her. He could tell by the deepening blush on her cheeks and the sparks of fire in her dark eyes. He'd tried telling himself all afternoon that this snippy waiflike creature couldn't possibly interest him. But here he was, ostensibly to claim his niece's tennis shoes.

"I didn't think you considered yourself my client," she replied as she backed into the room nevertheless, her hands smoothing down the fabric of her lab coat. There were several stains of fresh blood on it and a stethoscope stuck out of a side pocket.

Suddenly tennis shoes didn't seem important to him anymore. He wasn't sure *what* was important. All Rafe knew was that he had to be there. He'd never kissed a woman who barely came to his collarbone before. He'd never wanted to. But at that moment, that was about all he could think of. That and the possibility that he was going slightly nuts.

Chapter Four

Just the thought of kissing that delectable mouth made every muscle in Rafe's body tighten. Suddenly, he felt himself moving uninvited into the room, as if one of those higher powers his Aunt Mimi was always talking about had taken over. Kat must have felt something too, for she had splayed herself against a display case of flea powder in the manner of a silent-screen heroine about to be tied to railroad tracks. Not exactly flattering, Rafe remembered thinking before he moved even closer.

Then he moved closer still, allowing that sweet scent of hers to wrap around him. One hand reached out, encircled her neck, reveling in its silken coolness. He drew her to him. Her eyes, doelike, startled and questioning, met his. But Rafe had run out of answers. Kat—short, pert, sassy—not his type. Rafe's body disagreed: his pulse was racing, and his heart was hammering. Her lips had parted, and her breath was coming in sweet gasps. As her eyelids fluttered, he lowered his mouth to meet hers.

That was when he felt the sneeze come on. It must have slammed into him, for when he managed to look up, he was several feet from Kat. He tried to say something, but another sneeze exploded from him, only to be followed by a series of eruptions that made him feel like Mount St. Helens.

"Are you all right?" This time *she* was moving toward *him,* amusement flickering in her eyes.

"I'm . . . I'm . . . Damn!" Another sneeze.

"Gesundheit."

"Thanks." Knotting his handkerchief into a ball, he thrust it into his pocket. There was a tickle at the back of his throat; he refused to acknowledge it.

"Maybe you'd better sit down." Kat had taken him by the arm and was steering him toward the nearest chair.

"I'm perfectly all right," Rafe muttered, resolutely refusing her aid. He gave a sniff as another sneeze threatened him.

"You don't sound all right. In fact, you look a little . . . ill."

"Oh? Do you doctor humans as well as horses, cats, gerbils . . ." Whipping out his handkerchief, he managed to stifle the next sneeze.

"Sometimes," she replied sweetly.

"Resist the urge, because I don't believe in doctors." He loosened his tie, then ran a shaky hand through his hair. Good Lord, he couldn't remember when he'd felt this rotten. One minute he was hot with passion, and the next he was hot with God only knew what.

"Oh, I see." She was nodding her head in that infuriating way that was becoming familiar to him. "But if you don't believe in doctors, what do you do when you become really ill?"

"I don't become *really* ill." His eyes had started to burn and water, and the fine sheen of perspiration that was beading his forehead made a liar of him. "Don't have time for it," he added.

"Oh, you just become a little ill, right?" Her voice was tinged with sarcasm, but at the cool touch of her fingers to his brow, Rafe remembered his mother performing those same loving gestures from childhood. That had been years ago, he reminded himself as he jerked away from Kat. He had to get some air. His progress toward the door, however, was halted as something wrapped itself around his ankles.

Looking down, Rafe saw an enormous golden cat entangled between his feet. The creature gave a plaintiff meow, then threw itself tummy-up across the path.

"Oh, God, cats!" He managed to get out before another sneeze ripped through him.

"No. Just one cat. Well, one cat in here. Seven in the kennels. But this one is very sweet, despite his name."

"His name?" Rafe hardly recognized his voice. He sounded like an advertisement for Dristan.

"Killer!" The woman, bending down to pick up the mop of fur, suddenly sounded positively cheerful. "His real name is Prince Ivan. My nephews renamed him Killer, but he's really a puffball." She scrutinized Rafe, then slowly added, "You really don't like cats, do you?"

Rafe had known this woman spelled trouble, but didn't need his childhood allergy to prove it by acting up again.

"Nothing personal," he managed, wondering when the next sneeze was coming. "It's just that I'm—" Rafe cut himself off; just saying the word *allergic* made him feel weak and ineffectual. He had to get out of there, and he'd be damned if he'd tell her why. Later, when his head was clear, he'd figure out what to do.

There was only one other problem—both she and her *familiar* were blocking his way. "It's just that you're what?" Kat prodded, looking up at him as she stroked the animal's thick fur. Then, on a nimble step back, which catapulted Killer from her arms and onto Rafe's jacket, she surmised, "You're allergic!"

Killer dug his claws into Rafe, who stumbled forward. En masse Rafe and Kat crashed into a magazine rack, sending copies of *Cats Today* flying in all directions. Killer dashed from the room with a howl of injustice, leaving the humans to deal with the wreckage.

"Are you all right?" Rafe heard himself croak from his undignified position on the floor. Kat had landed practically on top of him, and even under the circumstances, the feel of her against him was quite stirring. He felt oddly like a condemned man at a feast. "Well, are you?"

"Am I what?" she asked on an unexpected gurgle of laughter.

"All right?" he repeated, wondering what the devil she found so funny. Reluctantly, he rose to his feet. That soft breath of hers against his cheek had replaced all thought of sneezes with more pleasurable pursuits.

"No broken bones," Kat replied, allowing herself to be pulled to her feet. "I am sorry about all that."

"We seem to have that sort of effect on each other." He was staring at her, still holding her hand, and he had a smile on his face. Kat thought of it as his *forget-everything-but-me* smile. It pulled at something deep within her; made her blood run like hot silver through her veins; made her want to forget everything and just float away on a cloud with him. But she wasn't ready to forget, Kat reminded herself. Besides, how could she forget what she couldn't remember in the first place?

"Dr. Racanelli, is everything okay? I heard such a racket that I . . . Oh, excuse me."

Yanking her hand from Rafe's, Kat turned a beet-red face to her assistant. "Everything's fine. Killer was just getting into mischief, and as you can see . . . but don't worry about it, I'll straighten up everything." Stepping even farther away from Rafe, she made hasty introductions, then waited until Annie had left the room before turning back to Rafe.

"My grandmother would say the stars caused this to happen," Kat said, clearly at a loss for words. Then, seeing the amused expression on his face, added, "You know, *astrology?* Nana says some things are just meant to happen."

"I'm familiar with the zodiac."

"That's right, you're an Aquarian." A devilish urge prompted Kat to add, "In case you hadn't guessed, I'm one of those pushy, take-charge Leos!"

"*Leo?* You're a Leo?" He looked as if he might sneeze again.

"That bad, huh? Don't tell me you're allergic to *them,* too?" Kat bit back the urge to laugh. Instead she gently said, "Hey, you haven't sneezed in five minutes. Maybe you're not allergic after all."

"Never said I was. That was your diagnosis, Dr. Racanelli."

"I'm a cat vet, remember?"

"You mean you're not going to tell me to take two aspirin and call you in the morning?"

Ignoring his volley, she merely said, "There are shots for allergies, you know." Seeing the frosty look he sent her, she quickly added, "It's not that big a deal."

"There's nothing wrong with me."

Not much! "Maybe you're coming down with that virus that's going around," she added helpfully, following him to the door.

"*If* I am coming down with anything, it all began when I came in here!"

"Well! Maybe it'll stop when you leave. Then again, maybe, like that black cloud you carry around, it's with you for life." Defiantly she stuck out her chin and gave him what she hoped was a blistering look.

"Black cloud?" he murmured. Then, feeling as if there were an invisible cord pulling him, Rafe moved toward her once again. He could no more have stopped himself than he could have kept the sun from rising.

"Yes, black cloud." Her eyes flashed up at him as she edged away.

As Rafe closed the space between them, he felt a searing heat from his body. Oh, how he yearned for the soft coolness of her touch.

Kat felt the heat, too, as she swallowed hard against the silky feelings that rushed through her. He was close, too close, and yet she needed it, wanted it. She could see his eyes were glassy, their pupils a blaze of blue. His high cheekbones were branded with fever and the five o'clock shadow that covered his jaw suddenly felt arousing against her neck. His lips, warm and coaxing, sent prickles of excitement through her.

Oh, God, he *did* know how to kiss! Teeth, tongue and lips made an inventory of her neck before moving slowly upward. It was hot and rough and wonderful. Despite all warning, Kat was completely taken off guard. Somewhere in the proceedings, her lab jacket had been discarded, giving Rafe's hands free access and a power over her that stilled her thoughts.

"Black cloud, huh?" he murmured in her ear. As one hand sifted through her hair and the other cupped her to him, he pressed her against his hunger.

Kat's own passion seared through her as his lips brushed teasingly over hers, inviting her to open up to him, threatening to bring down her house of cards. Somewhere in the dim recesses of her brain, she knew she stood on the top balcony of that fragile structure. She wanted to say something, anything, but his mouth, like a thief, stole the words as it worked its silent magic on her.

Then, without warning, and with an abruptness that snatched Kat's remaining breath away, he drew back, hands braced on either side of her, and looked intently into her eyes. Not a word was spoken. Only their ragged breathing broke the silence. A stretch of time filled with possibilities and the beating of two hearts.

As Kat attempted to corral her thoughts, an eternity marched by. She desperately wanted to make sense of what had just happened, but the buzz on her lips and the imprint of his hands brought her needs to the surface.

Tumbling and aching, confused and guilty. All Rafe could do was look at her as if she were an inanimate object. Kat gulped in more air, fervently wishing the ground would swallow her. She had let Rafe in, almost brazenly, and made a fool of herself in the process. But *why?* Why, at the least temptation, had she fallen under his spell? Even now she couldn't muster the words to break it. But she had to, despite the need and hunger, and all the memories of a love that had been true. Let Rafe practice his glassy stares on someone else!

Rafe saw the sudden flash of pain and anger in Kat's eyes. He felt her stiffen, and wished that he'd had more control over his urges. What the devil was wrong with him anyway? He didn't normally come on this strong, certainly not with someone like Kat Racanelli. *Allergies? Temporary madness?* Why hadn't he taken Eleanor Forbes up on her invitation, which he was certain included more than the promised sherry and nouvelle cuisine. More to the point, why was he dangling after this vet anyway? Suddenly he was too tired and sick to answer his own questions.

Sick? Never! Stressed out, maybe. Sure, that was it—he was just overworked.

"I'd better get going now," Rafe managed to say as a chill descended on him. Then, seeing a look of confusion cross Kat's face, he gestured toward the wall that had apparently been holding him up and added, "Sorry about my lapse of sanity back there."

"Oh?" Kat's eyes grew as flat and unreadable as stones. "That's right, you came for your niece's tennis shoes." Quickly skirting Rafe, she disappeared into what he presumed was the kennel area.

Another chill swept over him. God, what he wouldn't give to collapse into one of those nice, comfortable-looking waiting-room chairs. It was probably a good thing she tended cats instead of humans. Ten minutes in her little clinic had not only brought on some rare malady, but had also managed to bring out the latent Lothario in him. Once he got back to River Run he'd be just fine, he told himself, as he idly began thumbing through an issue of *Cats Today*.

"Good God," he muttered, staring at a color centerfold spread of a white Persian wearing an emerald collar. "Cat-mate of the Month?"

"I agree it is a little tacky," Kat commented as she reappeared, tennis shoes in hand. "But people can get awfully funny about their pets. Especially if they don't have children."

"I wouldn't know about either," Rafe heard himself practically growl.

"But you're pretty attached to your horses."

"They are racehorses. I'd be crazy to neglect them." He paused, then added on a more civil note, "Glad the shoes fit."

"Thank you for their use." Gingerly she handed them to him, then did another one of her nimble steps back. What did she think he had, the plague?

"Anytime," Rafe muttered as he headed once again for the door. Maybe he *did* have the plague. Whatever it was, it seemed to come in waves, and at the moment he felt in danger of drowning. "Good night, Dr. R."

Dr. R.? Kat stood quite still after he left, then slowly let the back of her hand brush against her lips. They tingled and tasted of him, and though this excited her, it scared her, too. It was the wrong time. He was the wrong man. Slowly her hand dropped to her side, only to rise again, a tight fist pressed against the sob that came. Sinking into a chair, Kat let the tears come. It wasn't the first time, and it wouldn't be the last.

But there *was* one thing she could do—avoid Rafe Sinclair at all costs.

By the time he got home, Rafe realized Kat was right. He *was* sick. Not allergic, but just plain ill. He had walked into her cat clinic a well man, relatively sane, and left with God knew what. A temperature of 101 degrees confirmed his illness, and as he crawled into bed, he had the fleeting memory of cool hands stroking his forehead.

Rafe reminded himself that he didn't get sick. His near-empty medicine chest attested to that fact. His last allergy attack had been when he was thirteen. That was the same year his mother died, and all the medicine in the world hadn't been able to cure her. That was also the year young Rafe Sinclair decided never to get sick again—at least not really sick.

Tonight Rafe knew he was really sick, and the mother who had nursed him through mumps, measles and allergy attacks wasn't there anymore. The woman his father subsequently married was one of those cool blondes who, although she set Rafe's adolescent standard of beauty, hadn't known the first thing about being a mother.

A phone call from Marty came at noon the next day while Kat was finishing up a routine exam. She was certain it had to do with Nightstar. But Kat was taken aback when Marty asked her to come over as soon as possible and see what she could do for Rafe.

"But I'm not a *doctor,*" she insisted, after listening to Marty's recitation of his brother's symptoms. "Surely he's got a regular physician." The fact that the closest Kat had gotten to a doctor since her plastic surgery was a yearly visit with her gynecologist was beside the point. Lots of people avoided doctors, but that didn't make it right.

"No, he doesn't have a doctor—"

"Oh. Doesn't believe in them, because he never gets sick, right?" She could almost see Marty smile.

"Something like that. But if you could just come over...I think it might do him good."

"Well . . . I suppose some herbal tea might help, although he probably won't drink it." Kat's brow puckered in thought as she mentally conjured up her grandmother's various remedies. "Okay, I'll be over shortly, but if he gives me any trouble, I'm gone."

After hanging up, Kat went into motion, collecting an assortment of home remedies, which even she had to admit looked suspiciously like something the witches in *Macbeth* might have used. Since it wasn't traditional medicine, maybe Mr. Sinclair might be more receptive. Especially since he *never* got sick.

"Pride," Kat muttered, as she slung the shopping bag of medicines onto the front seat of the truck. "You are one proud man, Rafe Sinclair." But she could deal with that, and she could certainly deal with him flat on his back...well, as long as she was upright.

As for last night, he was obviously influenced by fever. Kat preferred not to think of the *fever* that had possessed her. With any luck, maybe Rafe was too ill to remember anyway. The fact that the evening was emblazoned on her didn't help things one bit.

"Chemistry," she spit out the word in an attempt to dismiss all those tender feelings Rafe had exposed. After all, she certainly hadn't asked for this. Wasn't she perfectly happy minding her own business? Falling in love, marriage, children—that simply wasn't in the cards for her, and surely not with Rafe Sinclair.

She would offer her services to the intractable man, most likely have them refused and go on her way. That would be the end of it. Rafe could go back to his life and she would go back to hers.

Get a grip on yourself, girl! All he'd done was kiss her a couple of times; it wasn't as if he'd proposed marriage. The nearest he got to a bended knee was crashing into the magazine stand. She smiled at the memory. Besides, she was sure his proposal wouldn't include marriage anyway.

Still, just thinking about him made her heart beat double time. Crazy as it seemed, she hadn't felt such a wild rush since that motorcycle ride when she and Jack first met. But that was different—that was love. First love.

"And you're a fool to think it can happen twice," she muttered out loud. Jack was special, and Rafe was just... just... Oh, damn, she didn't know what he was! The one thing she knew was that since meeting him, she felt as if her carefully constructed life was going to split apart at the seams. Surely that wasn't in the stars, too?

As Kat pulled into the driveway at River Run, she let out a slow breath that ruffled her bangs. She had seen some pretty spectacular scenery in Pineboro, but the sheer beauty of these rolling green hills that tumbled into darkened glens spoke of fairy-tale magic and mysterious spells. Silver-surfaced ponds reflecting an enamel-blue sky were dotted with white geese and squawking ducks. On a distant hill, a half dozen sleek chestnut Thoroughbreds grazed contentedly. As far as the eye could see, white fences followed the dip and rise of land, all leading to the majestic stone house on the hill—Sinclair's Lair, Kat had dubbed it as she headed toward it.

A pleasant-faced domestic in a black uniform and starched apron answered the door. Somehow Kat had envisioned a taciturn butler would tend to the unpredictable Mr. Sinclair.

No sooner had she been ushered into the library than Marty appeared. Even in casual khaki pants and a blue pullover, he looked quite aristocratic and debonair.

"Thanks for dropping by, although I'm afraid our patient won't be exactly oozing gratitude." Gesturing toward the door, he led the way into the hall and up a spiral flight of stone steps. The second floor hallway, decorated with tapestries and brass wall sconces, had been lifted from another century, and although at odds with the modern decor, seemed right.

"Don't let the mummy case bother you," Marty said as he paused to give the eerie relic a knock. "Meet Nefertiti, one of Auntie's finds from her days in Egypt."

"I take it a museum has the actual mummy."

"Our aunt's husband was an Egyptologist, he never found the mummy. Lord knows how he managed to keep this." Giving a sharp rap on Rafe's door, he added, "If he seems a little testy, ignore it."

As if to prove the point, grumbling sounds were heard from the other side of the door.

"Maybe I should come back another time," Kat suggested as Marty swung open the door.

"Nonsense! Besides, this was actually his idea." Quickly backing out of the room, he added, "And being so, I'll leave you with your patient."

"That's right, Dr. R." Rafe's voice boomed out in the high-ceilinged room. "You might as well step right up and gloat."

"I didn't come to gloat," Kat said as matter-of-factly as possible. "You're sick, and—"

"Can't you doctors think of another word besides *sick,* or *ill?*"

"Indisposed?" Barely noticing her surroundings, her gaze zeroed in on her patient. He was propped up in the center of a queen-size brass bed surrounded by papers, books and other paraphernalia. His face was flushed, eyes glassier than the night before, and the five o'clock shadow had deepened to a faint reddish beard.

"Stressed out," he corrected with a look of satisfaction. Then, raking his hand through tufts of hair, he added, "What implements of torture are hidden in your little black bag?"

Kat bit down on her lower lip to keep from grinning. He might be stressed out, but his feistiness indicated he would be on the mend soon. There was even something oddly appealing and boyish about him—a far cry from her earlier impression of a rich playboy.

"Well?" he prodded, pushing himself up in bed, "Aren't you going to ask to see my tongue?"

"I suppose you'll want a lollipop when I go," Kat countered as she opened her bag.

"Not a bad idea." His eyes lit up and his lips broke into a particularly fetching smile. Kat blamed it on fever, and, pulling out a jar filled with liquid, began to shake it.

"Aren't you going to take my temperature?" he persisted. Then, pushing aside a ream of paper, he said, "Care to sit?"

"Thanks, but no thanks."

"Hey, where's the bedside manner doctors are famous for?"

"To begin with, I'm not a doctor—"

"Nor an equine vet, but then we've been through that dance before. So, let's get back to the bedside manner."

"Vets don't need one." Leaning over, she touched his forehead. It was hot. Her glance fell to the thermometer on his nightstand. Picking it up, she murmured, "One hundred and one?"

"That was last night." With an inward breath, Rafe remembered the feel of soft curves against him, the brush of lips on lips and the sigh that had swept through her. He might be feverish, but by God, he hadn't imagined that brief scene. Besides, who in their right mind would fantasize making love in a cat clinic?

"Drink this while it's hot," Kat said, pouring the broth into a cup.

"What is it?" She really was quite lovely, he thought, with those snapping brown eyes and that pixie hairdo.

"*Cat soup!* Now drink up."

At Rafe's look of distaste, she said, "It's a garlic fish broth."

"And along with the silver cross you're about to put around my neck it'll ward off vampires, right?" Rafe teased.

If only she'd step a little closer to his bed and brush those cool fingers against his brow once again.

"It's an old family recipe," Kat replied, easing the cup to his lips.

"From Transylvania." Rafe made a face. Then, taking the cup from Kat, he chugged it down.

"I'm going to leave the rest with your brother. You should have some at least three times a day." Recapping the jar, she shuffled around in her bag for the next item.

"This is some echinecea." Quickly she added, "It's an herbal extract. Take a dropperful three times a day—it's supposed to boost your immune system."

"No written guarantees?"

"Nothing is guaranteed in life."

"Except death and taxes." Rafe saw a fleeting look of pain cross her face, as if the cliché had touched some raw nerve.

She paused for a moment, then withdrawing a rolled-up white towel, said, "I did this once when I had bronchitis and it worked. Are you coughing much?"

"At night," he admitted. "But I'm really feeling better."

"That's good news coming from a man who never gets sick."

"I'll never live this down, will I?" He wanted to see that smile of hers again, but she seemed determined to keep their encounter business only.

"From the little I know about astrology, I'd never guess you're a Leo." Rafe had brushed all his papers to one side, as if that might magically propel her onto his bed. Despite his skepticism, he was beginning to like the fact that maybe she *was* the Leo lady who was supposed to sweep him off his feet. If so, she'd done a good job. But wasn't it the man who was supposed to sweep the woman off her feet? "You're so...efficient," he added.

"You didn't seem to think so when I delivered Nightstar's foal."

"That was different," he heard himself grumble. "Still, you're not much of a Leo."

"Oh, I'm not, huh?" She was wielding the rolled-up towel like a bat.

"According to my aunt, they're show-offs, and you're so..."

"Efficient," she reminded him. "That's my Virgo rising. We make good caretakers."

"But underneath lurks the glitter and glamour, or should I say the turquoise lace?" Rafe was rewarded by a twitch at the corners of her mouth.

"That was a bridesmaid's dress, it doesn't count. We're getting off the topic of my visit." Keeping her eyes downcast she continued fussing with the towel.

"Yep, Virgo rising always has a slot for everything."

"'A place for everything, and everything in its place,'" Kat quoted as she unfurled the towel.

"You know, I think you're getting better," she said, holding out the towel as if it were an offering.

"It must have been the garlic fish broth, but back to this everything-in-its-place routine. Just what the devil are you going to do with that thing?"

"Oh, this? I'm going to put it on your chest."

"On my chest?" Rafe could have thought of worse things and, from the flush on her cheeks, he had a feeling this was going to be pretty interesting. "What is it, a menthol rub?"

"No, a mustard plaster. Be sure and tell me if it burns too much."

"Good God! That's out of the Stone Age."

"Listen, Sinclair, it works."

Sinclair? Boy, where'd that come from? Rafe felt himself squirm. It was one thing to drink some witches' brew and swallow a few herbs, but this was a bit much. "What do I have to do?"

"Just take off your pajama top."

"With pleasure, my lady," Rafe murmured after a beat, as he reached for the buttons.

"Don't be ridiculous." Kat blushed in spite of herself. "You know perfectly well what I mean. And I'm not your *lady.*"

Chapter Five

"Are you sure you don't want to give me a rubdown before you apply that?" Rafe asked as he nonchalantly shrugged out of his pj top and flopped back against the pillows. A rather ludicrous grin was plastered on his face.

"You're not that sick," Kat replied in what she hoped was her most professional voice. Although the sheet covered most of him, the mere glimpse of Rafe's chest and bare arms was doing curious things to her insides. His muscles, smooth and well-defined, seemed to invite a caress.

"Oh? And I thought I was at death's door." As if to prove his point, Rafe rumbled out a cough.

"Who, *you?*" Snatching back the sheet covering his chest, Kat slapped the mustard plaster in place.

"You sure this thing isn't going to set me on fire?" he asked, neatly skirting the question.

"If it gets too hot, take it off. Though you'll find it really does help to break up congestion." Kat watched as Rafe peeked beneath one corner of the towel.

"I feel like a Reuben sandwich." Wrinkling up his nose, he added, "No dill pickle?"

"First it was lollipops and now dill pickles. Do I look like a vending machine?"

"Far from it."

Befuddled by the way his gaze swept over her, Kat averted her eyes and, fumbling in her black bag, pulled out a stethoscope. "I just want to listen to your lungs."

"Through this mud plaster?"

"*Mustard*. Given your high spirits, I'd say you've already snapped back."

"Oh, but I could go into a sneezing fit, or a coughing fit, or even a decline. I might need resuscitation—mouth to mouth."

In an attempt to ignore him, Kat stuck the stethoscope into her ears, then leaned over, listened to his chest. "Breathe," she instructed in a purposefully cool voice.

"Wasn't aware I'd stopped." He took in a gulp of pure springtime, and liking it immensely, took in more. Rafe couldn't remember when he'd enjoyed a woman's presence more. Surely it wasn't just the fever. She was close enough to touch, and the memory of the feel of her in his arms was enough to burst a thermometer. Heavy breathing was a cinch around her.

"You know, you're beginning to get the hang of this doctoring business, after all," Rafe said after another cough.

"I'm a vet," she reminded him with what he thought was the most delightful smile he'd ever seen.

"Does that make me an animal? Or are you simply non-discriminating?" Rafe, feeling a twinge of regret that she'd folded up her stethoscope, quickly added, "Any more tricks in your bag?"

"Not unless you need deworming." She brushed the back of her hand against his forehead. Her touch felt like cool silk to him.

"I could have told you that."

"Told me what?"

"That I was hot."

"Right."

"But you could cool me off...eventually." Was that a blush on her cheeks? And was it really possible that Rafe had never known a woman who blushed before?

"We could do a tofu plaster, I suppose," she said with an air of distraction.

"Tofu?"

"Yes. It's excellent at bringing down fevers."

"I thought it was something people ate." Rafe thumped his mustard-plastered chest. "Where would you put it?"

"On your forehead. But since I don't have any with me, we'll have to settle for cold washcloths. Does that door lead to your bathroom?"

"You must have X-ray vision."

"Just call me Super Woman." She tossed the comment over her shoulder.

"Bet you look good in a blue cape and tights. Linens are in the cabinet on the right as you go in, but then you probably know that." Rafe pushed himself up on one elbow and watched her shadow against the blue-and-white-striped wallpaper. "You Leos really are efficient," he said when she reappeared, basin and cloths in hand.

"Virgo rising, remember? Now rest back." Setting down the basin, Kat unfolded a wet cloth and laid it against his forehead.

"Bossy." His hand reached up and connected with hers. "But then that's Leo's big flaw." As she withdrew her hand, he felt an unfamiliar pang of sadness go through him.

"For a man, you know an awful lot about astrology," she said as she wrung out another cloth.

"My aunt's influence. She won't do anything without consulting her ephemeris."

"You're lucky it's just your aunt. My whole family is star crazed." A slow grin spread across her face. "And I guess that includes me, too."

"We'll have to go stargazing sometime. I've got a great telescope."

"Next to your etchings?"

"Hey, is that any way to talk to a sick man?"

"Somehow, Sinclair, you don't strike me as a man into the zodiac."

So, they were back to *Sinclair*, were they? "Well, *Racanelli*, there's a lot about me that might surprise you." At the slight lift of her eyebrows, Rafe pulled the cloth from his forehead and chuckled.

"You're feverish," Kat said, applying another cloth.

"What will I do without my angel of mercy?"

"Marty can sub for me."

"Some angel." Rafe felt himself sink deeper into the pillow. What a vision Kat Racanelli was—hands on hips, head tossed back—all accentuating the fullness of breasts beneath her burgundy pullover. God, how he would love to feel her against him. She must have read his thoughts, or perhaps the glimmer in his eyes gave him away, for she fastened her little black bag and slipped into her coat.

"I'll leave the magic potions with Marty on my way out." She paused in the doorway. "Any other patients I should check on before leaving?"

"Cuthbert could use a pat on the head," Rafe said on an unexpected yawn.

"He's a cat? No, of course not," she quickly corrected on a laugh.

"A black Great Dane, but hey, cats are all right. And despite what you think, I am not allergic to them."

"And you never get sick. Okay, okay! I'll give Cuthbert a pat. Get some rest."

No sooner had Kat left, than a wave of exhaustion swept over Rafe. Although bright sunshine splashed into the high-ceilinged room, he felt as if someone had just turned out the light and taken away the lush scent of spring—Kat's scent.

Pulling the washcloth from his forehead, he let out a groan. Forty-eight hours ago he hadn't even known Kat Racanelli existed, and now his whole life seemed focused around her. No woman had ever claimed that much space in his well-ordered, if somewhat unpredictable, life.

Fever. That would explain everything. Maybe when he recovered, all of this would make sense. But what would he feel about Kat then? Hell, it wasn't as if she were even interested in him. Of course, therein lay the rub, he mused somewhat poetically. If Kat were an Eleanor or Millicent type, he'd at least know how to deal with her. But she wasn't, and for all her blushes, and even their brief scene last night, he knew it was a dead-end course. They were worlds apart.

Worlds apart...or were they? Despite Rafe's social track record, there was that other side of him that few people knew existed.

Struggling to keep awake, he wondered what Kat would think if she knew that River Run Stables had a volunteer horse-therapy program for disabled children. Rafe was a soft touch where those kids were concerned. He loved working with them. There were even times when it seemed the children were the most important thing in his life.

But telling Kat about his other world would probably look like noblesse oblige. Best to keep it to himself for now, Rafe counseled himself as sleep closed in on him.

* * *

Kat should have been hungry, but she wasn't. It was probably just as well, she decided, glancing at the time as she pulled into her drive. Although she'd spent almost an hour with Rafe, it seemed like ten minutes. However, Kat didn't want to think about that—and she certainly didn't want to think about the way he made her feel. Swinging the truck door closed, she headed up the flagstoned path to the clinic.

Feelings. Immediately after Jack's death there had been none. Since she'd returned to Pineboro and set up practice, there hadn't been time for any. At least that was what she'd told herself. Deep inside she knew that wasn't the real reason.

The reason was simple—fear. Kat had loved once and death had snatched that love from her. If it happened once, it could happen again. If it happened again, she wasn't sure there would be *any* feelings left at all.

Kat paused on the porch, face turned toward the disk of pale winter sun, and remembered the way Rafe had held her, remembered how the heat from his body had sent chills through hers. Chills that turned to fire. Flames that licked at all those frozen feelings.

Feelings that were still there—vulnerable, fresh and aching with a need she'd thought long buried. It was as if that same energy that pushed crocuses through winter snow were also pulsating through her and piercing her protective armor. Like those early spring flowers, she felt as if she were being pushed through frozen ground to face the sun again.

However, it was too soon.

Entering the clinic, Kat resolved to stop thinking about Rafe and what he did or didn't do to her. Thankfully she had a busy afternoon ahead of her: two spay operations and a teeth-cleaning session with one of her least favorite patients, a temperamental Siamese. Still, dealing with even the most difficult cat was easier than dealing with the unpredictable Sinclair.

Sinclair? She'd called him that, simply let it pop right out of her mouth. But Kat didn't do things like that—never had, except with Jack, and then it was a term of endearment. Which could hardly be the case with Rafe. Their relationship was just chemistry. Passion perhaps, but certainly not love. Not on his part, at any rate.

Getting ready for surgery, Kat mulled this over even more. After all, in college she'd met plenty of jocks who went from one conquest to another without an iota of tenderness or responsibility. Well, maybe Rafe wasn't exactly a jock, but he wasn't Mr. Sensitivity, either. Making a face at her ridiculous title for him, she snapped on her surgical gloves, put Rafe out of her mind again and turned her attention to the operation.

By the end of the afternoon, Kat once again felt in control of her life. No tumultuous roller-coaster emotions or flights of fantasy assailed her. Her feet were on the ground and her boundaries were in place.

However, her first clue that things weren't as peachy-keen as she'd thought was the fact that she was humming snatches of Simon and Garfunkel's "I Am a Rock"—a far cry from her earlier crocus metaphor. Her second clue was that, despite her enthusiastic rendition of the song, she felt slightly numb—as if *she* were the one who'd breathed gas, not the cats. And the cat that should have been knocked out, namely the ill-tempered Siamese, hadn't been. Even with her assistant holding him down, the feline had managed to drag his claws across Kat's hand just before sinking his teeth into her thumb. At least they were freshly cleaned teeth, Kat had mused, and although her emotions were somewhat numbed, her hand certainly wasn't.

She was cleaning out the cat bite when her sister Tonia burst through the door with a dozen long-stemmed red roses. "For you!" she said, whipping them past Kat's nose on her way toward the kitchen sink. "Oh, did one of your clients claw you again?"

"Patients," Kat corrected, sidling up to her sister to get a look at the card.

"It says, 'Love and kisses, your devoted servant, etc., etc.'" Tonia informed her as she retrieved a vase from the cupboard and began filling it with water.

"Oh, it does not," Kat rejoined, snatching the card from her. "And I can't imagine who would be sending me flowers anyway...." She paused to read the note.

"I'd say a very happy client. I don't think it was for a spay job. You know you really ought to put something on that gash. What were you treating, a mountain lion?"

"It really *does* say 'Love and Kisses'—"

"Don't forget the 'devoted servant' part," Tonia said, plopping the roses into a fluted-glass vase. "Of course I haven't met him, but his brother's pretty interesting. Hey, did I do a flower arrangement or what?"

"Wait a minute! Slow down! Whose brother?" Kat snapped the small card between her thumb and index finger.

"The devoted servant's brother. These will look beautiful on your bedroom mantel," Tonia murmured as she headed for the stairs, Kat following in her wake.

"Devoted my foot!—you don't mean...oh, it can't be..." Kat practically tripped on the bottom step.

"Fast work, Sherlock! And all for delivering a foal and putting mustard on Rafe's chest. Whoa, that must have been fun." Reaching the top of the steps, Tonia continued undeterred to Kat's room.

"I did what anyone would do in that situation."

"Correction, Sis. A couple of Tylenol tablets and some cough syrup is what *most* people would do. Or maybe an antibiotic—"

"Antibiotics don't do a thing for viruses."

"Cool down. Marty said you're the best thing that's happened to his brother in years."

"Marty talks too much!"

"With that accent, I could listen to him read the telephone book all day."

"Oh, come on!"

"Well, he does have a certain charm, but I can see the Sinclair boys are lost on you." Turning from the mantel, Tonia added, "See how nicely the roses pick up that deep red in your Oriental carpet?"

"I'm in a swoon," Kat said, tossing her hands in the air, only to plant them firmly on her hips. "Now if I've followed this correctly, Marty—"

"Yes, Martin Sinclair." Tonia's voice went up an octave, reminding Kat of the way she used to murmur Paul McCartney's name when she was in grade school.

"Okay. Martin must have come over to the restaurant with these . . . these flowers."

"Roses! And right before Valentine's Day."

"Oh, Tonia. You're supposed to be the levelheaded member of the family. You're sounding like Nana or Maria, instead of . . . of . . . *the rock!*" Kat sniffed, as if this sudden blossoming on Tonia's part had betrayed a trust.

"I am not a rock," her sister countered. "I have feelings, just like anyone else."

"Of course you do. What I meant was . . . oh, damn! I'm too confused to know what I meant. Except that I certainly didn't expect you to fall in love with Rafe's brother. You . . . you just met him!"

Ignoring Kat's comment, Tonia shifted her attention back to rearranging the roses. "He came by the restaurant as I was going off the lunch shift. He wanted to make sure you got these."

"Okay, so instead of doing the logical thing, and bringing them here, he took them to Rosa Motta's." Kat gave an impatient shrug to her shoulders. "No doubt Rafe, in his delirium, gave Marty that address."

"Not exactly..." Tonia's face lit up like a sparkler on the Fourth of July. Kat suddenly felt ashamed for pooh-poohing her burst of emotion. Just because *her* emotions were doused, that didn't give Kat an excuse to throw a wet blanket on her sister's.

Softening her curiosity by lowering her voice, Kat sat on the edge of her bed, with hands clasped tightly around the love-and-kisses card as if it were a winning lottery ticket. "Okay, so what's the real reason he came to the restaurant?"

"He said that Rafe had raved about the manicotti, so he stopped to try it. He also came back to congratulate the chef—yours truly—the modest one." Tonia grinned. "Anyway, one thing led to another—"

"What do you mean, 'one thing led to another'?"

"Oh, just that we have a date for tonight, tomorrow night and Saturday night."

"I see. Grass certainly doesn't grow beneath *his* feet." After a beat Kat added, "So why not a date on Friday night?"

"Some sort of family function he's got to attend. Oh, he asked me, but I'd rather wait awhile before meeting his family." Sitting beside Kat, she gave her sister a playful nudge. "Don't say it. I know this is all a bit crazy."

"Okay. My lips are sealed on that subject. Back to the roses!"

"Simple. When he discovered we were sisters, he asked if I'd drop them off. Maybe he thought they'd be better received from me."

"Florists do deliver. Or perhaps that was too prosaic for Rafe."

"Hey, pull in your claws, Kat. After all, 'a rose is a rose is a rose.'" Crossing to the mantel, and plucking one of the flowers from the vase, she dropped it in Kat's lap. "He even had the thorns removed!"

"Okay, okay. Point taken. But that doesn't mean the man walks on water." Kat plunked the rose back into the vase.

"No. Probably just skis on it." Tonia's smile took up her entire face. "Well, I'd better get ready for tonight. We're kicking up our heels at that new dance club on West Broad." Pausing on her way out, she added, "Too bad Rafe is sick and can't go with us. Martin says he's a regular Fred Astaire. Toodle-oo!"

"Well, I'm not Ginger Rogers!" Kat called after her, feeling unaccountably irritated. They were beautiful roses, and no one, not even Jack, had ever sent her a dozen of the long-stemmed beauties. Chewing on her lower lip, she pondered what to do. Call and thank him? Write a note? Or thank him the next time she saw him? But Kat didn't want there to be a *next time*—or did she?

The jangle of her phone saved her from further ruminations. It was Nana, reminding her about the hostess job at Mrs. Chandler's on Friday. Well, she thought as she replaced the receiver, that's one evening I won't be obsessed with Rafe.

Buoyed by this thought, Kat went downstairs, fed Killer, fixed herself some supper, then wrote Rafe a brief thank-you note. A last-minute inspiration struck, and she included one of her Garfield comic strips. Let him gnaw on that, she thought, hurrying out to mail it before changing her mind.

No sooner had the envelope slipped down the chute than she muttered curses. Why was she wasting her time on him? Although not one to read the bumper crop of How to Land a Man manuals, Kat knew by osmosis what their opinion of this situation would be. Did they also take into account that empty feeling inside her? Or her need for a man's touch? Not just *any man,* she thought, wiping away an unexpected tear that rolled down her cheek.

Rafe was not just any man. Unfortunately though, he probably thought of her as just another woman. A conquest worthy of a dozen red roses?

On impulse, Kat decided to go to a movie, a funny one. If she was going to keep her sanity, she'd have to stop thinking about Rafe.

It worked. She couldn't remember when she'd laughed so hard. The next night she corralled a friend for a Japanese horror movie featuring giant caterpillars vs. Godzilla. It was the perfect remedy for anything.

When the hostess job at Mrs. Chandler's rolled around the following evening, Kat considered herself cured of *Sinclairitis.* Rafe had hardly entered her thoughts, except for when she'd read "Garfield" that morning.

She thought of him again that evening when she slipped into the red silk dress for her hostess duty that night. Briefly, she wondered what he'd think of her in the clingy number with the rhinestone straps. The bolero jacket covered a lot less of her than she'd remembered, leaving quite a bit on display. She considered changing, but there wasn't time. As for the vague warning bell in her head, she completely brushed that aside.

Nana had given Kat the River Road address. Nana didn't, however, tell her it was a reconstructed British castle, complete with a gate house and keeper! He was a friendly sort and, after getting her name, opened the massive wrought-iron gate and waved her through.

Kat slowed the truck to a crawl as she navigated the steep graveled path to the top of what appeared to be one of Richmond's seven hills! The setting sun sent shafts of scarlet through ancient magnolias, and prisms pierced the turreted structure that sat like royalty on a throne. It was definitely a castle, and from the looks of it, authentic.

Kat had gleaned her knowledge of history from novels and old movies, and yearned to catch a glimpse of Errol Flynn and Olivia De Havilland. It was the romantic in her, or as Nana would say, her Leo Sun challenging the Virgo rising. The eternal romantic vs. the pragmatist.

Still wrapped in mists of the past, Kat parked in a designated spot, and slowly made her way to the front door. *Door* wasn't quite the right word for it. *Portal,* perhaps. It was made of scarred oak, with elaborate iron hinges and a knocker, placed high-up and fashioned for a giant's hand. Kat, standing on tiptoes to reach it, felt a little like Alice in Wonderland.

An amiable-looking, though definitely elderly man answered the resounding summons. He made a bow, and with a sweep of his hand, welcomed her. Kat, following him into a side parlor, imagined him to be the loyal family retainer.

After he left, she made a leisurely perusal of the antique-filled room. Shards of twilight slipped through mullioned windows, and a pewter chandelier cast a warm glow over the rest of the room. A unicorn tapestry covered one wall; a sea chest with brass fittings and two carved chairs were directly in front of it. On the other side of the room was a cherry sideboard, with a highly polished surface that shimmered like glass. A crystal vase on it held an arrangement of roses and baby's breath, and while the lingering scent was heavenly, it reminded Kat of Rafe.

Rafe, roses, Valentine's Day. Today was Valentine's Day, and it was just like any other day, or so Kat had tried to tell herself. Then why the empty feeling? Turning away from the flowers, her gaze fell on a suit of armor, standing arrow-straight, guarding the door. The combination of closed visor and poised ax sent a little shiver through her.

A mummy case, propped in a corner, caught her attention. Moving toward it for a closer inspection, Kat couldn't help but wonder what Mrs. Chandler was like.

"You needn't fear, it's as empty as the other three."

Kat, startled by the voice, spun around. It had to be Mrs. Chandler herself. Her black-and-white designer suit and her upsweep of snow-white hair made her the personification of elegance.

"You see, I don't much hold with keeping the actual mummy." A warm laugh punctuated this comment as the woman entered the room, and extending her hand, she added, "I'm Mrs. Chandler, but please call me Mimi." Not giving Kat time to catch her breath, Mimi began chatting quite gaily about how efficiently Kat's brother, Gustavo, was handling the catering. Before she knew what was happening, Mimi had drawn her into the great hall.

"Now I want you to feel free to rearrange to your heart's content. Although the maid cleaned today, I'm afraid things are a bit crowded." Vaguely gesturing toward an even larger mummy case, she added, "I should have sent him to the attic years ago, but he was the first one my husband and I found, so he's become part of the family."

"You and your husband *found* him?" Kat's gaze swept from the enormous mummy case to the rest of the room, which looked like an overstocked museum. Every conceivable surface held innumerable treasures. The thought of moving any of them made Kat nervous.

"My husband was an archaeologist, and naturally we spent time in Egypt. He was so cracked on the subject of mummies that he insisted on being buried in one of the cases we found. Ah, but I mustn't go on so. You young people aren't interested in such morbid subjects."

Kat was casting about for some polite comment concerning mummies when Mimi said, "I'll just go get Greeves to help you move some of the larger pieces." Checking her watch, she added, "We have plenty of time before the guests arrive, although my nephew is so unpredictable, there's no telling when he'll show up."

"Oh?" Kat digested this fact before continuing, "He's not coming with his parents?"

"It's a *surprise* birthday party. He thinks he's coming over to check out a leak in my roof."

"A leak in your roof?"

"I told him that my yard man was having trouble finding the leak." Switching subjects in a manner that reminded Kat of Tonia, she said, "Maybe if you just scoot Ramses to the other side of the room—"

"You have a very large roof, and it's dark out." Kat paused, hoping she hadn't overstepped her bounds.

"Heavens, I'm not *really* going to send the lad to the roof. Besides, there is no leak." Mimi's gaze strayed back to Ramses.

"But isn't he going to be suspicious?"

"Oh, my dear child, no! He's an Aquarian. They're in a fog half the time—"

"I thought that was Pisces," Kat interjected, following Mimi's gaze as it zipped around the room.

"Pisces are in a fog *all* the time," the older woman said on a soft laugh; then, delicately patting her chest, she added, "I should know, that's my sign." Kindly blue eyes crinkled into a warm smile. "But then you'd know about astrology, wouldn't you? Well, I'll just get Greeves so we can clear some space for cake and ice cream.''

Kat opened her mouth to say something. Just what, she wasn't sure. It wouldn't have mattered anyway; Mimi was drifting toward the door.

Making a quick inspection of the Great Hall, Kat decided to take matters into her own hands. Besides, she suspected Greeves was the kindly but ancient butler, hardly a match for Ramses. Within minutes, her suspicions were proven correct. He arrived with two maids and asked what they might do to help. When she suggested that they clear off the various tables, they seemed relieved. Obviously they wanted no part of Ramses's mummy case.

Kat, not too eager to wrestle with it either, pitched in and helped them—which was probably a good thing. No sooner had they finished than the florist arrived with baskets of flowers. At least there was space for them.

When a five-piece band descended on them, she was clearly puzzled. She thought it a bit odd for a teenager's birthday party. The flowers seemed slightly funereal, especially when added to Ramses's macabre presence. However, the band, merrily tuning up, practically suggested a wedding. My, she thought, how the eccentric wealthy did pamper their offspring! Oh, well.

Ramses definitely had to be moved to a less conspicuous place. Egypt perhaps? Or at least across the room. He shouldn't be too hard to move, Kat reasoned as she wrapped her arms around the weather-beaten wood and made an attempt to inch it across the tile floor. Progress was steady, but very slow. The fact that she couldn't see where she was going made it tough sledding indeed.

The band's warm-up rendition of the Beatles' ''I Want to Hold Your Hand'' had given Kat the needed impetus in her trek across the room. She had reached the halfway point, directly under the chandelier, when she collided with something, or someone. Steadying the mummy case, she dropped her hands to her sides, stepped back and turned around.

"Rafe! What are you doing here?"

"I could ask the same thing," he replied, suddenly feeling mildly annoyed with what was obviously a ploy on his aunt's part to throw them together. She'd been trying to make matches for him since he was eighteen. He'd have to have a chat with her.

How Kat fit in was a mystery, but Rafe was even more curious as to why the devil she was dragging that damn mummy case across the floor. He'd known his aunt was planning a surprise party for him. As usual, there were the flowers and the band. But Kat Racanelli?

Although her mustard plaster had worked, he'd been trying to write off his growing attraction to her as hormonal, or at least as a side effect of the fever. It wasn't. He had completely recovered, and she looked more luscious than ever. That left hormones to blame.

"What the dickens are you doing *here?*" God, she was lovely. He felt the ache inside him grow.

"I'm practicing cat burglary!" As lightning flashed in her dark eyes, Rafe wondered what they looked like when they smoldered with passion. But it was more than passion that he wanted to see reflected in those eyes.

Rafe had always kept women at arm's length. Whether they were friends or lovers, he'd held back. But tonight, on his thirtieth birthday, he wanted it to be different. In a heartbeat, he knew it was Kat who would make that difference.

It was Kat he wanted and, contrary to the Beatles song, he wanted to do more than just hold her hand.

Chapter Six

As "I Want to Hold Your Hand" ended, the band tried a bit of "The Tennessee Waltz." A tune made for slow dancing—one that pulled at heartstrings and memories. Rafe had always liked the song but, at this particular moment, it made him feel as if he were in some damn three-handkerchief movie. It underscored his needs. It was Kat he wanted all right. But perversity drove him to say, "Cat burglary? Well, you're doing a lousy job of it."

"I can see you've recovered from your illness," she said in an airy voice, as she wrapped herself around the mummy case. "And now, if you'll excuse me, I'll continue with my job."

"Let me," Rafe interjected in a gruff voice. "You'll ruin your... your dress." Stepping between her and the case, he couldn't help but notice the lush expanse of pale olive skin against the scoop of scarlet silk that covered her breasts. The pleasurable ache in Rafe's stomach tightened to a knot. He swallowed against this feeling, then pivoting the mummy case on its side, said, ''I take it you were heading for that far wall?''

''Oh, no. I was going for the roof and a fast getaway.''

Though Rafe couldn't see her, he sensed the smile on her face and, above the music, heard the humor in her voice. It made him feel lighter, as if there wasn't anything he couldn't accomplish. Anything except moving the damn mummy across the room. Ramses wasn't exactly a feather. After having moved it countless times over the years for his aunt, he knew that. How on earth Miss Half-Pint managed to heft it at all was another of those mysteries that seemed to surround her.

Her latest appearance at his aunt's aroused Rafe's curiosity even more. He wanted to grill Mimi, but knew she'd tell him that his obsessive nosiness was just another example of Aquarian eccentricity. Nevertheless, his aunt would have some explaining to do.

''You made it.'' Kat's voice sounded chipper as Rafe managed to shove Ramses against the wall.

''I don't always smash into things,'' he murmured, then turning to face her, he leaned against the mummy. ''I'm still wondering at my good fortune in finding you here.''

''The wonder is shared,'' Kat replied, her eyes fastened steadily on his. ''You know this *is* a children's birthday party. I can't help but wonder why you'd want to crash it.''

''I'm just a big meanie.'' At Kat's amused expression, he added, ''I get my kicks from popping toddlers' balloons.''

''You're out of luck. I gather Mrs. Chandler's nephew has graduated from Romper Room.''

''Oh, so I'm crashing a teen scene?'' Rafe pushed away from the mummy and casually brushed past Kat. Electricity charged the air. ''Mrs. C. certainly is putting out the red carpet for her nephew.''

"*Mrs. C.?* Really, Rafe!" Kat swung around to face him. "You still haven't explained what you're doing here."

"Ditto, Half-Pint." Rafe liked the way that made her eyes snap. But then, he was liking almost everything about her these days.

"*Half-Pint?*" she echoed.

"You'd rather be called Jumbo?" His lips twitched in amusement.

"Neither, thanks." As she shifted from one foot to the other, Rafe couldn't help but notice the way her silk dress molded itself to her hips and thighs. He yearned to reach out and stroke the length of her. Maybe later, if the music was right, they'd get to dance.

"I suppose I could go back to calling you Dr. Racanelli. Oh, by the way, the mustard bit worked. Actually, I was impressed that it cleared things up in two days."

"Glad to hear it...oh, and...and the flowers were beautiful."

"So you said in your note. However, as much as I'd like to take credit for them, I can't." Rafe thrust his hands into the pockets of his slacks. "That is, I can't *remember* sending them, though given my feverish spasm, perhaps I did." He couldn't resist a smile. "I vaguely remember doing some other rather heated activities."

"Let's just say you weren't yourself." A becoming flush stole over Kat's face. "As for the roses—"

"Roses, was it?"

"A dozen...long stemmed. And since your name was attached to the card, I thought that..." Kat paused as awareness dawned on her. Of course, it had to have been Marty's idea. But why?

"And just in time for Valentine's Day." Pivoting from Kat, he added, "Since you seem to be on a secret mission for my aunt, I'll just have to track her down and find out what's cooking myself.''

"Your aunt? *You're* Mrs. Chandler's nephew?''

"The same. You know, the one who graduated from Romper Room.'' He pressed that maddening smile on her, then, turning, headed for the door.

"Wait a minute!'' she cried, catching him by the arm. "Then it's *your* birthday. But I thought...that is...'' Releasing her hold on him, she stepped back.

"Pretty excessive, isn't it?'' Rafe's gesture took in the flowers, band and refreshments.

"But...but you're not supposed to be here. It's a surprise.''

"Aunt Mimi's been throwing these surprise birthday parties for me for some time.''

"Doesn't your mother feel a little left out of it?'' Almost immediately Kat knew she'd trespassed. Quickly she tacked on, "I'm sorry. It's none of my business.''

"Don't worry about it. My Mom died when I was thirteen. My Aunt Mimi was her older sister, and she sort of stepped in to help Dad.''

"Oh...I'm sorry, I didn't know.'' Kat had a sudden glimpse of a sad little rich boy. Not arrogant, spoiled or lazy as she'd first thought, but a lonely, hurting and perhaps angry child. Knowing this was going to make it even harder to keep Rafe at arm's length. But keep him there, she must.

"Well,'' Kat managed at last, "I might as well tell you that I'm here to help run the catering.'' Glancing at the sideboard of refreshments, she added, "And if I want my brother to speak to me again, I'd better get to the kitchen.''

"Allow me to lead the way,'' Rafe said, linking arms with her.

His touch set off a tingling sensation, almost as potent as those fiery kisses of his. Just thinking about them made her feel plugged into a high-voltage socket. Then hadn't Nana often referred to Aquarians as walking lightning rods? Well, that was great for them—they obviously thrived on being shocked. Kat, however, wasn't quite that well-grounded.

By the time they'd threaded their way to the kitchen, she'd managed to regain her composure. Disengaging her arm from his, Kat told herself that lightning never strikes twice in the same spot. Then, after a cursory introduction to her brother, she gave Rafe a shove in the direction of the hall.

"This is supposed to be a surprise!" Kat whispered, trying her best to be stern, but the boyish look of innocence brought a laugh to her lips.

"And it will be," Rafe promised as he patted her cheek. "I've yet to let Aunt Mimi down."

"Then get out of the kitchen!"

"Don't tell me—you're going to jump out of my cake and do a cancan on the table. Right?"

"Wrong!" Biting on her lower lip to keep from laughing, she said, "Are you going to go or not?"

"Not!" Pulling a stool under him, he sat down, crossed his arms over his chest and grinned at her. "Aquarians are very stubborn."

"Obviously. Why?"

"Mimi says it's because we're *fixed air.*"

"I know that." As her brother zipped by with a tray of hors d'oeuvres, Kat lowered her voice. "I mean, why are you posting yourself in the kitchen? Do you think I'm going to walk off with the pots and pans?"

"You were the one who brought up cat burglary." Rocking back on the stool, he eyed Kat through narrowed eyes.

"Very well, if you want to spoil the surprise your aunt has planned, suit yourself." She started to move past him, but he caught her by the arm.

"Promise me a dance, and I'll disappear."

"That's blackmail," Kat protested, fighting down the ripple of pleasure his interest caused. "But okay, if you'll just get out of here!"

"Such tender sentiments." With deliberate languidness, Rafe eased himself off the stool. "Any requests for the band?"

Kat cocked her head to one side, and remembering Tonia's comment about Rafe being a regular Fred Astaire, said, "'The Continental.' Or is that too far back in the Stone Age for them?"

Rafe let out a laugh. "When you finish in the kitchen, put on your dancing shoes and, as they used to say, we'll cut the rug."

Kat, feeling slightly disoriented, stared into space a full minute after Rafe disappeared. Every nerve in her body was charged. If she'd been in the dark, she'd undoubtedly have glowed.

"Basta!" Scooping up the nearest tray of finger sandwiches, she headed for the Great Hall. Surely a single dance wouldn't hurt, she told herself.

A half hour later the place was buzzing with more than one hundred guests. The women were decked out in glittery gowns—sequins, rhinestones and a smattering of real jewels; most of the men wore suits and ties, but Kat counted more than a dozen men in formal wear. Since her job was to circulate and make sure everyone was fed and watered, it was pretty easy to keep tabs on the guests.

The party was in full swing when Marty arrived. From the surprised look on his face when he spotted Kat, she knew *he* knew that Tonia had told her about them.

"Well, you could knock me over with a feather," he said as he reached her. Then, lifting a glass of champagne off her tray, he added, "You are the most multitalented woman I've ever met. I gather you're hostessing and not doctoring. By the by, how's your latest patient?''

"Rafe?" Kat shot Marty a questioning look. "He's the picture of health. Although ... he seems to have a memory lapse concerning sending those roses."

Marty's eyebrows lifted. "Found me out, did you? Well, they had to be sent and, since Rafe wasn't in any condition to tend to it, I did. I've appointed myself the lad's social secretary."

"Oh? I had no idea his calendar was so jammed."

"I'm working on freeing it up just a bit," Marty said, taking a sip of champagne. "But then what's an older brother for anyway?"

"Stirring up trouble!" Rafe said with a laugh as he came up behind them. Then, removing the tray from Kat's hands, he added, "Come on, there's someone I want to introduce you to."

"Hey, what's this, fraternizing with the help?" Kat made a halfhearted attempt at reclaiming her hand.

"It's Fred and Ginger hour!"

"*This* I want to see," Marty murmured, as he trailed behind them.

"What if I turn out to have two left feet?" Kat tried for a casual tone, a sort of counterpoint to the drumming of her heart.

As Rafe stopped short, Kat tumbled into him. He merely chuckled and giving her hand a squeeze, said, "Then I'll try not to step on them, but since they're Munchkin feet, I wouldn't worry about it."

"*Munchkin?*"

"The little people in Oz," he whispered. Then, with a tug on her hand, he added in a normal voice, "Thought you might like to meet my dad. Damn, he was right here a minute ago. He's been disappearing on me all night."

"Maybe he thinks you're still contagious," Kat offered with a straight face.

"You didn't catch anything, did you?"

Kat looked up at Rafe and, feeling her heart do an odd little lurch, lied. "Not a thing."

"Hey, that's our tune," Rafe said, as he laced his long fingers through hers. " 'The Continental,' remember?"

She wanted to protest, to go back to the safety of doling out champagne and hors d'oeuvres—but it was too late. No sooner had they reached the edge of the dance floor than Rafe had encircled her in his arms. For the space of a moment he pressed her against the length of him. He was lean and hard where she was soft and full; his tweed jacket felt rough and exciting against her silk dress; his heartbeat seemed to echo hers; the soft explosion of his breath against her cheeks made her feel a dizzying surge of pleasure.

Then they were dancing, no, more like gliding effortlessly across the floor. It was an intoxicating, heady feeling, almost as if they *were* Astaire and Rogers. One dance, just one simple dance, Kat told herself.

Rafe couldn't remember the last time he'd danced. Probably with Millicent at their engagement party. She hadn't really enjoyed it, preferring instead to sip Chardonnay and talk about the round of parties they'd attended. Rafe couldn't imagine Kat doing that. Kat, his Munchkin, his Miss Half-Pint.

Rafe almost missed a beat—*his?* The word, like a thief in the night, had slipped into his brain. When had it all begun anyway? Somewhere between that foggy night in his driveway and this moment on the dance floor, he'd come to think of her as *his*. Kat was everything Millicent and all the others weren't; where they were cool, she was warm, witty, womanly and down-to-earth.

As he watched her twirl to the music, a memory of his mother came to mind. Like Kat, she had been small with dark hair and merry brown eyes, high-spirited and generous. Was it then that Rafe had decided to pursue Snow Queens? It would have seemed safe to love them; for, unlike his mother, those remote Amazons were indestructible. There was only one problem—Rafe had never loved any of them.

As Kat whirled back into his arms, he felt a resurgence of spring coupled with an exuberance that made him feel that, like Fred Astaire, he probably *could* dance on ceilings. Looking into Kat's eyes, he saw an inner light he'd missed before. Her guard was down. It was then that Rafe realized that perhaps she, too, carried around a ghost from the past.

"Happy Valentine's Day," Rafe murmured, as the music came to a close. Then holding her in his arms, he teasingly said, "Don't I get a kiss?"

"I think you've overdosed in that department, Sinclair." There was a ribbon of laughter in her voice, though once again her eyes were veiled.

"Hey, there's no such thing as overdosing on kisses." With the flick of his finger, Rafe tilted her chin and, looking deeply into her eyes, tried to read their hidden message. She blinked her lids as if she were being interrogated under hot lights.

"Well, I suppose since it's your birthday—"

He leaned into the kiss, then with surprising restraint, merely brushed his lips against hers. They parted and quivered beneath his, sending a passionate longing through him. His fingers tightened their hold on the soft flesh of her upper arms.

On a steadying breath, Kat stepped from the circle of his embrace. The touch of his lips was as hot as a firebrand, and desire pulsated through her. Kat took in another deep breath. She needed to get away and think. She hadn't wanted this relationship, and yet there it was. "Happy Birthday," she managed to say after a beat.

"Thanks." His word, soft and low, swept across her like a caress.

Kat swallowed against the feelings that seemed to blossom at the sound of his voice. "I'd better get back to work. There are a lot of hungry and thirsty people out there."

"Better keep those cucumber sandwiches circulating."

"Right," she replied on a salute. Turning, she made her way toward the kitchen. Her brother, who was arranging a tray of antipasto, looked up as she entered.

"You've certainly had your hands full this evening." He paused, the dark Racanelli eyes scoping her out. Like Kat, he was small and compact with olive skin and a shock of jet-black hair. "Well?" he prodded. "What's with you and the rich birthday boy?"

"C'mon, Gus, don't be so class conscious. He's really quite nice...for a jet-setting playboy." Busying herself with loading up the sandwich tray, she bit down on a grin.

"Oh, then he *is* a jet-setter?"

"Yes, and he'll undoubtedly whisk me off to Bora Bora."

Seeing the brotherly concern in Gus's face, Kat quickly added, "Relax. He's okay."

"I remember how you used to feel about the rich country set." Gus made a sweeping gesture with his chopping knife. "And I doubt if they come much richer than this. Did you know that in the thirties this castle was taken apart stone by stone and then shipped over from England to be reconstructed on River Road?"

"No, but I'm not surprised," Kat replied with some impatience. "But getting back to my views on the rich, they're changing." She paused to decorate the platter with several sprigs of parsley. "And times have changed, too, haven't they?"

"You're still a Racanelli," Gus reminded her, "and not a Temple-Smythe."

"Hey, Big Bro, I don't need a lecture on my roots. My memory's fine, and you needn't worry about Rafe Sinclair. I'm not the least bit interested in him." With a sandwich tray in hand, Kat started for the door, hoping that Gus didn't see the slap of color on her cheeks.

"You could have fooled me," Gus said, picking up the antipasto tray and following Kat to the Great Hall. "Just don't do anything rash, Sis."

Kat paused in the doorway. Why was it everyone in her family seemed determined to live her life for her? "I never do things rashly." Jutting out her chin, she walked briskly into the hall. What did Gus know, anyway? If she wanted to have a friendship with Rafe, she would. Period. Kat did not like to be told how to run her life, and certainly not whom to fall in love with. Besides, she didn't love Rafe, and certainly wasn't about to do anything rash. On entering the Great Hall, however, she felt a pang at not seeing him. The band was playing "The Tennessee Waltz," and suddenly Kat wanted to dance.

From his position across the room, Rafe had a clear view of Kat. She looked vulnerable and very appealing. He realized his Aunt Mimi had been on target for once. Whether it was the stars or just plain chemistry, Rafe was undeniably attracted to Kat. Attracted? Hell, more like *magnetized*.

"What do you think of our hostess, Miss Racanelli?" his aunt asked, joining him.

"Efficient." Rafe clipped out the word, then slowly gave his aunt a sideways glance. "I know what you're up to, old girl."

"I don't know what you're talking about," Mimi protested. "Miss Racanelli is doing an excellent job."

"It's *Dr.* Racanelli."

"Dr., is it?" Mimi purred. "Oh, yes, Marty mentioned something about her treating Nightstar. By the way, I got a postcard from Carla asking about the mare. She's coming home early; seems that Peggy's business deal is going to take longer than anticipated. So you'd better get her room ready."

Relieved that the subject had switched from Kat to his sister Peggy and niece Carla, Rafe felt himself relax. He'd do anything for those two; they'd always been special to him. But after the car accident that had claimed his brother-in-law's life and had almost crippled his six-year-old niece, Rafe had grown even closer to Carla and Peggy. "I guess the first thing she'll be wanting to do is ride."

Mimi smiled up at her nephew. "If it hadn't been for those horses of yours, I doubt she'd even be walking today."

"We'll never know." Out of the corner of his eye he saw his father approaching Kat. Torn between going over and catching their conversation, or trying to get some information out of his matchmaking aunt, he chose the latter.

"So, Auntie, why don't you and I have a little chat about the stars." Steering her toward a bank of chairs against the far wall, he could see that Mimi was clearly flustered by the fact that his father was carrying on an animated conversation with Kat.

"So, what's Dad up to?" Rafe asked without preamble.

"Oh, you know your father," Mimi replied with a wave of her hand. "Mind you, I'm very fond of my brother-in-law, but . . ."

"But what?"

"Well...we all know he's a little eccentric...and it really is a shame he didn't stick with Broadway...."

Rafe nodded his head. "Right—but let's fast-forward to the present. What's Dad up to now?"

"It's just a silly muddle, but if I tell you what he said, promise me you won't go off half-cocked."

"It's a promise. Besides, I never do things halfway. So what's up?"

Kat wasn't sure whether to believe the man or not. There was something charming and offbeat about him, but she was certain he was telling a tall tale about his supposed nephew. Why the whole world suddenly felt a moral obligation to ply Kat with advice concerning Rafe was beyond her.

Her latest adviser was tall and thin with a mustache that reminded her of Groucho Marx. He'd introduced himself as Rafe's Uncle Willy from Topeka, and within the space of ten minutes he'd not only managed to extract most of her life story but had informed her that Rafe's wealth had all the eligible women after him.

"I pity the poor girl who marries him," he said in a stage whisper.

"You think he'll beat her?" Kat countered in conspiratorial tones. "Or perhaps you're just referring to debtor's prison." She watched closely as Uncle Willy nodded his head solemnly. The man was just a bit out to lunch, although quite sweet. But why was he going on so about Rafe?

"He's a good boy, if a little batty," Willy informed her as he tweaked his mustache in the manner of a silent movie actor.

"But a poor boy," Kat finished for him. "And you're just sort of warning me, right?"

"Correct, Miss Racanelli. But it's his mental state that says it all."

"A lunatic?" Kat suggested, biting back a smile. Whoever Uncle Willy was, he certainly had Rafe's interests at heart. Rafe—*crazy?*

"Perhaps that was a bit strong...."

"Well, put your fears to rest. I have absolutely no designs on your...nephew...is it?"

Uncle Willy's gaze softened. "No designs?"

"Not even if he owned Fort Knox." Kat watched as his face crumpled slightly.

"Well, perhaps Mimi and her eccentric friend are right," Willy said.

"I beg your pardon?"

"Mimi and her friend Rosa...are cracked on the stars. They've been plotting this romance for months. I told Mimi this astrological mating stuff was a lot of nonsense, but... Excuse me, my dear." With another tweak of his mustache and a military bow, Uncle Willy turned and disappeared into the crowd.

Mimi Chandler and Nana? Who else would he have meant? Kat felt her cheeks burn at the thought of their conspiracy. Then of course there was also Tonia and Marty trying to stir up the brew. With a fluttery sigh that ruffled her bangs, she added her brother Gus to the growing list of family busybodies. With Gus on the opposite side, Kat was beginning to feel like the piece of rope in a tug-of-war game. Only for her this was not a game. Kat felt exposed and vulnerable, as if all those tender feelings she'd thought to be dead were not only alive, but under public scrutiny as well. She wished she could turn invisible, but meeting Rafe's heated gaze as he approached her, she knew that avenue was closed.

Taking in a deep breath, she realized she'd discarded her bolero jacket, and was standing in the middle of the dance floor in the red silk dress with the rhinestone straps. At this point, invisibility was out of the question.

Chapter Seven

Whatever Rafe had been thinking practically shot out of his head. Just the sight of Kat in the shimmering red silk dress scrambled his thoughts. Though with her flushed cheeks and rapid breathing, he wondered just what his father had said to her.

Mimi moved past Rafe and linked arms with Kat. "So what did you think of Rafe's father?"

"*That* was Rafe's father?" Kat blinked dramatically.

"Whatever he said," Rafe put in, "you can discount it on general principles."

"But he said such glowing things about you," Kat protested. Then cocking her head to one side, she added, "Though I must admit I was a trifle surprised to learn you'd been in Oak Haven Rest Home."

"I shall strangle him!" Mimi announced. "But first he'll apologize for being so...so..."

"Oh, you needn't," Kat said, catching hold of Mimi's hand. "He was really quite sweet. I think he imagined that I was a fortune hunter, and that—"

"And that I was the door prize," Rafe tacked on with a laugh. So, his father had been at it again.

"Door prize, huh? Did Oak Haven let you out for your birthday?"

"They always do," Rafe replied, as he slipped an arm around Kat's waist and nudged her toward the dance floor.

"There are times when I think Barton's the one who belongs in Oak Haven!" Mimi's eyes narrowed to dangerous slits. "As if Rosa and I didn't know what we were doing. And I'm going to have a little chat about that right now."

"I really do think your father is a dear," Kat said as Rafe pulled her into his arms. Although she should be annoyed with her grandmother and Mimi, she really couldn't get cross with them. The picture of them hatching the matchmaking was actually both amusing and touching. As for Rafe, Kat wasn't sure what she felt—but there was certainly magic in the air. Maybe it was the strains of "The Tennessee Waltz," or the way Rafe's hand glided around her waist. Maybe it was the nearness of him, the beating of his heart or the tangy smell of his after-shave. But when Rafe began softly singing along with the music, Kat felt herself melting into the strong arms that encircled her.

"Do you know the words?" he asked, tightening his hold on her.

"Bits and pieces. I think the song predates us by a good ten years." She offered him a tentative smile. Even though everything about Rafe felt good, Kat still couldn't quite trust her feelings. After all, her deep love for Jack hadn't kept fate from dealing its blow.

Rafe drew Kat even closer. "What are you doing tomorrow night?"

She tightened up almost immediately. And what made it even worse was the fact that there really wasn't a single reason for the reaction—at least nothing that made any sense. She tried to write him off as an arrogant playboy, but knew better now. The more she understood him, and the more she liked him, the more frightened she became.

Forebodings and nightmares? How on earth could she explain to Rafe, or any other man for that matter, that when it came to intimacy she felt as if she were sinking into quicksand?

"Well," he prompted as the song came to an end, "can you take a break from your cats, or will they mutiny?"

The sparkle in his eyes momentarily swept her fears to one side. "Only one of them is my cat."

"Killer."

"Yes, the ferocious attack cat." Kat let out a laugh. There was no getting around it, there really was something delightful about Rafe.

"About tomorrow night—I know this nice little restaurant in Shockoe Bottom that has the best mussels in town."

"Thanks, but I really can't." Kat, averting his gaze, added, "You see, my felines just might mutiny."

"I might also," Rafe said on a chuckle. "You know how we Aquarians are."

"Unpredictable!"

"And," he continued, "persistent."

"Are you trying to reinforce to me that you're stubborn?"

"You could say that." As Rafe closed the distance between them, Kat's heart speeded up. The dangerous smile that lurked at the corners of his mouth seemed a prelude to a kiss. She feared his kisses were as addictive as potato chips—impossible to have just one. As far as Kat was concerned, the man should come with a warning from the surgeon general: "Rafe Sinclair is suspected of being responsible for heart palpitations in susceptible females."

"So, how about dinner at this new jazz club?"

"I don't like jazz," Kat replied breezily. "And right now, I'd better get back to work."

"How about fifties rock?" Rafe asked, following her to the kitchen.

"That was before my time," she tossed over her shoulder.

"So was 'The Continental.'"

"And 'The Tennessee Waltz,'" she reminded him playfully. Turning around at the kitchen door, she added, "Actually, I have some major surgery scheduled early the following morning, so I'm going to have to take a rain check. I'll try to remember the part about you being persistent."

"I'll remind you," Rafe said with a wink before he blended back into the party.

The cleanup went a lot faster than Kat had expected, but then her mind was on other things. The band had stopped playing, yet the strains of the music echoed in her ears. Her hands were busy with a thousand tasks, yet the feel of Rafe's callused palm against hers sent a tingle down her arm. Her earlier fears, temporarily put to sleep, were replaced by a delicious feeling of weightlessness.

The party had just about broken up, and Kat was headed out to their catering van when a stunning blonde, loaded down with packages, came in the front door. Depositing a sack worthy of Santa Claus on the sideboard, she gave Rafe an embrace. Then, gesturing toward the packages, she said something that made Rafe laugh.

Kat felt her cheeks turn bright red. How silly she'd been to take Rafe's flirtation seriously, when it was obvious he had a girlfriend—several, in fact. What had she expected anyway? That a wealthy, aristocratic Sinclair of Pineboro County would be seriously interested in the granddaughter of Italian immigrants? It appeared that Gus was right. Reminding herself that a tiger never changes his stripes, Kat slipped out the side entrance. Thankfully the van was packed and she could leave.

As she descended the steep driveway that led to Mimi Chandler's castle, Kat wondered just how her grandmother and Rafe's aunt managed to get together. And why on earth did they think that Rafe and she would make a perfect couple? Undoubtedly earth had nothing to do with it: more likely the collision of heavenly bodies.

Seeing the elegant blonde kiss Rafe had disturbed Kat more than she knew. She'd been sure she would fall fast asleep that night, but her mind chewed over the evening's incidents until even herbal tea and a boring murder mystery didn't put her to sleep.

She finally dozed off around three o'clock, only to be awakened by her recurring nightmare—the stable fire. Thankfully it wasn't as disturbing or vivid as it had been in the past. Still, Kat awoke trembling. Killer, who always slept at the foot of the bed, had positioned himself inches from her face and was consoling her by pawing her cheek and making mewling sounds.

"Oh, Killer," she cried, dragging the warm, fluffy body into her arms. "I'm really all right. It was just another bad dream. Someday I won't have that dream." After rocking the cat for a moment, she let him go. Then, rolling onto her side, she stared out the window at the starry sky. Eventually a dreamless sleep came.

The next day Kat had clients scheduled back to back and, although she hadn't had enough sleep, adrenaline kept her going. When the last animal had been tended to, and her assistant had gone home, a mild depression settled in. The antidote was simple—go to the movies, eat some popcorn and don't think about Rafe. Kat also decided to stop off at the bookstore and pick up another mystery. The only real glitch in the weekend was going to be the traditional Sunday dinner at Nana's. The entire tribe would be there and, given the sudden interest in Kat's love life, things would undoubtedly get sticky. Besides, Kat had a few words to say to Nana. But that was tomorrow, and this was tonight— show time!

She just had time to duck into the bookstore before the feature started. It was one of her favorites, *A Night at the Opera*, and she didn't want to miss the opening.

Kat had gotten her mystery fix and was headed for the checkout when she spotted Rafe's tall blonde browsing in an aisle marked *Weddings, Etiquette, Personal Growth*. Feeling decidedly uneasy, she leaned against the counter and slowly pulled a five-dollar bill out of her wallet.

As the sales clerk rang up her sale, Kat stole another look at the woman. She was thumbing through what had to be an expensive bridal book. From the looks of her tan suede coat, she could probably afford any item in the book. She was a very attractive young woman, with shoulder-length honey-blond hair and only a hint of makeup. The woman fit right in with the country-club set—Rafe's set—the kind of people Kat had envied all her life. With an inward sigh, she collected her purchase and headed into the mall. Obviously, she still envied them.

By the time the movie was over, the Marx Brothers had restored Kat's sense of equilibrium. Later that evening, the new murder mystery made her practically forget that she'd ever met Rafe Sinclair. However, just as she was about to drop off to sleep, she had a jarring image of Rafe and his blond bride walking down the aisle. Kat's eyes flew open. *No!* That had to be all wrong. How could she be Rafe's type? The Rafe she'd come to know *wasn't* the jet-setting playboy.

With a groan, Kat rolled onto her side. He might not be the obnoxious, bored rich kid, but he was definitely a rich kid! And Kat was from the wrong side of the tracks; the only way *old money* crossed those tracks was first class or club car. The wealthy usually married the wealthy—only in movies like *The Prince and the Showgirl* did the pauper heroine get her millionaire.

Right before falling asleep, Kat made a mental note to ask her grandmother if the stars took that into account.

The following morning brought deceptively balmy weather. An enamel-blue sky with its puffy white clouds looked like a page from a child's fairy tale. It was perfect weather for Rafe's kids. Every Sunday, except in the most inclement weather, the children gathered at River Run Stables for their horse therapy. Unless he was away on business, Rafe would usually stop in and chat with them. And despite his preoccupation with Kat, this morning was no exception.

By the time he reached the small ring where the children rode, they had already gone through several sets of exercises. On seeing their Uncle Rafe, all four of them screamed their greetings in unison.

The youngest in the therapy program was Stevie, a five-year-old boy who'd been born with a rare congenital muscle weakness. The others included seven-year-old Megan, whose drug-addicted mother had left her slightly retarded; eight-year-old Paul, who'd been battling muscular dystrophy for three years; and ten-year-old Andrea, a survivor of spinal meningitis. Despite their handicaps, they were all cheerful, spirited children determined to overcome their disabilities.

Rafe leaned on the split rail fence that enclosed the paddock and waved back at his kids. Although this latest group had been in the therapy program for only two months, Rafe felt a close bond with them. Ever since he'd begun the program, there had been a kinship with the children. The love and growing trust they showed for the horses was somehow heartening to him; though few people knew it, it was actually the children who were teaching Rafe to open up.

"Uncle Rafe!" Carla, sitting proud and erect on her chestnut mare, approached the fence. It was almost impossible to believe that six years ago the doctors had said she'd never walk again. But they hadn't taken into account her love for her uncle's horses, nor had they known how determined she was.

"Belated Happy Birthday!" Carla said, drawing gently on the reins. Her blue eyes were sparkling and her tawny-colored hair blew in the wind. Gesturing toward the attractive blonde who was working with the children, she added, "I'm sorry I missed the party, but Gwen said it was a lot of fun, and that the kids had her bring you a sack full of presents from them."

"I guess you could say I cleaned up," Rafe said with affection. "Two Nintendo games, a purple striped tie and a stuffed orangutan."

"Just what you need!" An impish smile lighted in her eyes, "Well, don't you want to know what I got you?" Beckoning for Rafe to follow, she nudged the horse around and headed for the barn.

"Close your eyes," she instructed as they entered the building. "It's not wrapped, and I bet you still can't guess what it is."

"A racehorse!"

"Nope."

"A saddle with silver trim?" Rafe felt a childish urge to peek.

"Wrong!" Carla's voice floated down from the loft. What the dickens would be up there? Rafe wondered. "No fair peeking, Uncle Rafe."

"The suspense is killing me," he teased back.

"Hold on," she replied in a breathless voice as she hurried down the ladder. "Okay, hold out your hands."

Doing as he was told, Rafe felt an enormous fur ball being gently deposited into his hands. Looking down, he saw what had to be the largest, most ferocious tomcat in the world staring back at him. Oddly enough, he was purring, which Rafe supposed was some consolation. Calling him homely would have been a kindness. In the cat-world Mafia, he'd undoubtedly be called Scarface. One of his ears was half-gone, the other one was thoroughly chewed, and his gray tabby coat, although well brushed, looked as if someone had used the animal for BB target practice. In his favor, however, aside from the rumbling purr, he had beautiful green eyes flecked with gold.

"I named him Scruffy." Carla looked expectantly at Rafe. "I got him a really neat rhinestone collar, and his own comb and brush and a carpet tree house, 'cause he's such a sweet little kitty."

"Little?" Rafe shifted the laconic animal from one arm to other. "Scruffy belongs in the *Guinness Book of World Records*." Skeptically regarding the cat, he added, "Where did you find this eighth wonder, anyway?"

"By the side of the road in a canvas sack!" With a toss of her head, she added, "I'll never understand how anyone can be so cruel to their animals."

"There are all kinds of people in this world, honey, but luckily for him, there are people like you." Stroking the cat elicited a silent meow. "You know, Carla, I have a feeling old Scruff and I are going to get along just fine. Thanks for my surprise gift."

"Oh, I'm so glad you like him!" She paused, then softly added, "I haven't had a chance to get his shots yet, but there's a really nice vet on Kennebeck Road. I met her when our kitty had to go in." Carla's eyes danced with mischievous delight. "She's only been in Pineboro a few months and she's real pretty, too."

"I think I know who you mean," Rafe said, as an image of Kat in the red silk dress rose up before him. Kat... just thinking about her sent ripples of pleasure through him.

"Dr. Racanelli," Carla confirmed as she headed for the stall to retrieve her horse. "Have you met her?"

"Yes—"

"Pretty, isn't she?" Carla reappeared, leading the mare by the bridle.

"Listen, young lady, I don't need you joining forces with Aunt Mimi on this. But to answer your question, yes, Dr. Racanelli is quite attractive."

"Oh, so Auntie's been doing a little matchmaking! By the stars, no doubt." Swinging herself into the saddle, Carla made an unnerving appraisal of Rafe. "You need a change from all those tall, frosty blondes."

"Right. And you think Kat—Dr. Racanelli—is the perfect antidote?"

"So it's Kat, is it?" With another very grown-up toss of her head, Carla urged the mare forward.

"It's actually Katrina," Rafe put in, feeling unaccountably bested. He followed his niece from the barn.

"A pretty name for a pretty lady," she replied, pausing at the edge of the paddock. "And if you don't give me a full report at dinner, then I'm sure Uncle Marty will."

"Don't forget Aunt Mimi," Rafe muttered, wondering why he was feeling as if his script had just been yanked from his hands. Scruffy, displeased with being dragged into bright sunlight, dug his claws into Rafe's black bomber jacket and let out a yowl.

"He's probably hungry," his niece informed him.

"Well, forget it, Two Ton," Rafe said, prying the cat loose from his death grip on the jacket. "Because you're about to go on a diet." Scruffy let out a pensive meow that came out sounding like "Now? Right now?"

"Yes, *now,* you hedonist!"

"Oh, that reminds me, I also got him ten pounds of diet cat food 'cause he is a little bit overweight." When Rafe merely nodded, Carla quickly tacked on, "But Dr. Racanelli should probably check him out before you do anything drastic."

"Oh? I don't think a ten-day water fast would be too drastic for our furry friend."

"Uncle Rafe!"

"Just joking, Carla." Hoisting Scruffy onto his shoulder, he felt as if he should probably burp the enormous creature.

Within minutes Gwen and the children had gathered around him and the cat. A chorus of "nice kitty" filled the air as eager hands reached out to stroke Scruffy.

By the end of the afternoon the children had a new mascot, and Rafe discovered that his childhood allergy to cats was apparently gone. He also found himself more attached to Two Ton than he could have imagined. Although the elasticized rhinestone collar looked ridiculous on Scruff, it was the hot-pink food mat printed with *The Cat's Meow* that really tickled Rafe. Carla had gone all out for this abandoned alley cat. But then his sixteen-year-old niece was a believer in lost causes—extending to and including her bachelor uncle.

Midway through dinner, after she had pumped every ounce of information out of Marty, Carla suggested that they invite Dr. Racanelli over to meet Scruffy.

"After all, she came over to deliver Nightstar's foal," Carla said triumphantly. "And from what you said, she did a super job."

"Yes," Rafe conceded, "but as a rule, vets don't make house calls. Besides, there's absolutely nothing wrong with Two Ton."

"Scruffy," Carla reminded him gently.

"There's nothing wrong with Scruffy that a diet won't cure."

"Got to think of the shots, old man," Marty put in as he pushed his salad bowl to one side.

"I'll make an appointment tomorrow morning." Catching the conspiratorial look exchanged between his brother and niece, Rafe added, "So you two can stop plotting." What they didn't know wouldn't hurt them, he reasoned. That way, he'd at least save face if things didn't turn out the way he had hoped. Even though Kat still wasn't exactly showing interest in him, that *would* change. After all, hadn't he told her he was persistent?

Lovely Kat Racanelli. What was it about her that made her so skittish about men? A bad marriage? A husband who'd beaten her? God, he didn't want to think about that. Though he'd told his niece that there were some pretty mean people out in the world, the kind that abandon animals and beat wives, the thought of anyone laying a finger on Kat made Rafe's blood boil.

"Penny for your thoughts," Marty said. "You look like you're about to strangle someone."

"The light in here's lousy," Rafe replied smoothly. "As for Scruff, he'll have his shots first thing tomorrow, *and* I suppose we could have Dr. Racanelli over for dinner one night next week."

"That's more like it!" Carla cried.

"Or, as the saying goes, *now* you're cooking with gas." Marty poured himself a cup of coffee and, resting back in his chair, gave his brother a wink.

Rafe returned the gesture, wondering if his brother read him as well as he thought he did. His interest in Kat was there—no denying it—but was Rafe the only one who'd seen those flashes of fear in her dark eyes? Somehow he would get through and dispel whatever lurked there. For there was one thing Rafe knew for sure—Kat Racanelli had captured his heart in a way no other woman ever had. All Rafe needed to do now was to capture hers as well. She'd called him unpredictable. Wouldn't she be surprised when she found out just how unpredictable he could be!

Sunday evening dinner of the Mottas and Racanellis was an affair that began shortly after noon Mass and seemed to continue well into the evening. It was a tradition, had been in the Old Country, with each succeeding generation of Americans adding on to it.

Since Kat's parents were vacationing in Florida, the meal was a little more subdued. Nevertheless, Rosa made sure her *famiglia* was well fed. Lasagna, as the main course, was supplemented by asparagus with hollandaise, baby carrots in a gingered sauce, smoked salmon on sourdough biscuits, a sparkling green salad and almond cookies with banana pudding for dessert.

"Katrina, a little more pudding?" Without waiting for a reply, Rosa started to spoon more into her dish.

"Whoa, I've had enough!" Kat's hand quickly covered the dish. "And it was delicious, though I wonder how I'll get out of this chair, much less back home."

Refilling her own bowl, Rosa resumed her seat. "Such a happy gathering. All my grandchildren but Maria are here. Ah, but she's off on her honeymoon...." Casting a pointed look in Kat's direction, she added, "At least one of you had the sense to get married!"

"Shirley and I don't count?" Gus asked, giving his wife's hand an affectionate pat.

"You are a man, that's different," Rosa said with a sniff.

"She's referring to us women," Tonia put in as she finished the last of her pudding. "We're the unmarried lot."

"Old maids," Elena, the youngest, said with a giggle.

"Correction," Kat said. "Having been married cancels that status. I'm a widow." Although she felt a slight twinge at using the word in such a cavalier manner, there was something oddly freeing about it.

"Widow, old maid, spinster! It all amounts to the same thing. My beautiful granddaughters are not married, and this is not natural."

"Now, Nana, this *is* the 1990s. A woman's identity doesn't depend on having a husband." Kat instinctively felt the third finger of her left hand. Even though she'd removed the simple gold band several months ago, she still toyed with the slight indentation on that finger.

"Times have changed indeed," her grandmother muttered. "What I want to know is, what will become of the family without husbands and wives and bambinos?" Looking to her grandson, she added, "It's all going to fall on Gustavo?"

"Well, he is the male Racanelli," Elena pointed out as she rose and began clearing the table. "He's also a wonderful dishwasher." With a wink, she indicated that he should help her in the kitchen.

As if on cue, everyone but Rosa got up to help.

"Katrina, *vieni qui!*" Patting the seat next to her, Rosa said, "Come, tell me how your job with Mrs. Chandler was. Did you meet anyone interesting?"

"I was going to get to that, Nana." Resuming her seat, Kat tried to give her grandmother a stern look, but seeing the attempted look of innocence on her face, she gave up. "You've been at it again, haven't you?"

"At what?" Her eyes blinked in mock surprise.

"Matchmaking!"

"*Matchmaking?*" Rosa applied herself to the banana pudding with renewed fervor.

"Yes, you and Mimi Chandler have been tinkering with the stars, and with Rafe and me." Kat tried to suppress the smile that threatened to crack her face.

"Oh, that!" Rosa licked the spoon clean, then carefully placed it alongside her dish. "He's such a nice young man and so successful at his job."

"*Nice* isn't the first adjective that leaps to mind—successful, yes. *Determined,* yes..." Kat took a breath. She really didn't want to think about just how determined he was.

"And an Aquarian." Rosa dropped this reminder as if it were the definitive piece of evidence tipping the scale in his favor. "He liked you, yes?"

"Frankly, I think I'm just another woman, a notch on his belt." Crimson color stained her cheeks as the memory of his kisses pressed against her lips.

"What is this expression, 'notch on his belt'?"

"Oh, Nana, it's too hard to explain. I don't care what the star charts say, we're not meant for each other!"

"Ah, *perfetto!* What is that English saying?" Rosa knit her brow in thought, then snapping her plump fingers, said, " 'The lady doth protest too much, methinks!' "

"Shakespeare wrote that. But I'm not protesting too much. I'm simply protesting a little." Running her thumbnail along the edge of the dining-room table, Kat averted her eyes.

"A little, a lot! Still it tells me you care. But I knew that, for your Moon is on his Sun, and Venus and Mars in the composite are trine—"

"Nana, I don't care if they're spinning out of orbit—"

"If you're not careful, you'll be the one spinning out of orbit." As Rosa pushed away from the table, she gave Kat a long steady look. "Don't be so quick to throw away what the stars have given you."

"Nana, I'm not throwing anything away. I'm just being sensible about the whole thing. I'm not his type...." Kat paused, only too aware that she was fast becoming his type.

"You are frightened, that is all, bambina. It will pass. Everything does." She gathered up the remaining dishes on the table before adding, "But you are right about one thing: I *am* an interfering busybody, and Mimi and I did set up the party. *But* we didn't arrange the planets. Someone who knows a lot more than we do can take the credit for that."

Kat watched her grandmother disappear into the kitchen and felt a sudden sense of loneliness descend upon her. Why couldn't she just break with the past, forgive herself for what she couldn't remember and get on with her life? The fact that Nana and her star charts might be right troubled her deeply. Was it possible that she was throwing happiness away with both hands? Something told her that Rafe was the kind of man who'd be there for the long haul. If only she could open up to him, at least for longer than a few kisses and a dance.

Chapter Eight

The morning hadn't been going well at all. Usually Mondays were the slowest days at the clinic, but the springlike weather seemed to bring everyone to Kat's door. There were the usual complaints—necessary shots to be given, and several emergency procedures. Just when Kat thought she and Annie could sit down for a quick lunch, Rafe entered the clinic, accompanied by a tearful teenage girl.

"He was hit by a car!" the girl blurted out. "Please do something for him!"

"Follow me," Kat said without preamble as she led them into an examining room.

"It looks pretty bad." Rafe gently deposited the carrier on a stainless steel table. "We think it happened about an hour ago. My niece found him by the mailbox."

Kat eased the injured cat out and made a quick examination of him. Hooking up an IV, she said, "He's in shock, but at least he hasn't lost too much blood. Still, he'll need fluids before I can operate."

"Operate?" Rafe asked, feeling hopelessly inadequate.

"I'm pretty sure he's got a broken hip, but I'm going to x-ray him to see how bad it is." Inserting the IV, Kat adjusted the drip for maximum effect. "I've put a sedative into it, so I can go ahead and x-ray him." Looking up at Rafe for the first time, she said, "What's the little fellow's name?"

"Little?"

"Well, you know what I mean." Kat stroked the animal's fur, taking care to avoid the abrasion. In a few minutes he'd be calm enough to x-ray.

"Scruffy, also known as Two Ton. Carla gave him to me for my birthday."

"And then some horrible person hit him and left him to die!" Carla blotted her eyes with her knotted-up hankie.

"Well, unless I'm mistaken, this is one tough tomcat, and he's not about to die." Kat offered the girl a reassuring smile. Reaching up, Kat pulled down an X-ray machine and positioned it over the cat. Gesturing toward a small cubicle, she said, "Step behind that lead shield while I take a picture of him."

"But he's so quiet," Carla said as she followed Kat and Rafe to the cubicle.

"The sedative's working fast. It's really okay." Normally cat owners didn't observe this end of the examination, but somehow Kat knew it was the right thing to do, especially for the girl. She had to admit, however, that this was a side of Rafe she hadn't expected to see. Obviously he was *not* allergic to cats anymore. She couldn't say why, but this pleased her.

The X ray showed a compound fracture, requiring immediate and rather extensive surgery. Although both Carla and Rafe seemed determined to stay, Kat finally convinced them that since it might take a while, they'd be more comfortable at home.

As she'd suspected, the operation took several hours. It was a nasty break, requiring a pin. On the positive side, however, the old tom had a great constitution and would make a speedy recovery. He would also undoubtedly lose some weight!

By the time she'd finished stitching him up, it was practically three o'clock, and she was starving. Wanting to keep an eye on Scruffy, Kat told Annie to go to lunch without her. There were leftovers in the fridge that would tide her over until dinner time. She'd just pulled out some three-day-old minestrone and a loaf of questionable rye bread and was at the point of phoning Rafe when he and Carla appeared loaded down with Chinese carryout.

"Can we see him?" Carla asked as she deposited one of the bags on the kitchen counter.

"Sure thing. He's still pretty groggy," Kat said as she led the way to the kennels. Although they only stayed with Scruffy for a few minutes, it was obvious that the visit put both Carla *and* Rafe at ease.

The Chinese carryout was spicy and delicious. No sooner had they finished it, then another cat client in need of shots arrived. While Carla made a last-minute visit with Scruffy, Rafe pulled out his checkbook to pay for the operation.

"I seem to remember your not wanting my check last time." Rafe smiled. "Something about not taking money under false pretenses."

"I recall that phrase." Kat smiled up at Rafe. "I was pretty obnoxious, wasn't I?"

"And I walk on water, right?" After hastily making out the check, he handed it to her. "Now don't give me a hard time about the amount. After all, you did deliver Nightstar's foal."

"But Rafe, this is too much!"

"Shh!" Tilting his head to indicate the new patient in the reception area, Rafe added, "And that's just a down payment. Tomorrow night I'd like to take you to Atlantic City, just for the fun of it, okay?"

"But Rafe—"

"Your spirits need a little buoying up. Of course, I'm not a medical man, but that's my prescription, nevertheless."

"But I don't gamble," Kat protested, as she fingered the hefty check in her hand.

"Well, maybe you should start. After all, what's life without a few risks? You know what they say—"

"No, but I'm sure you're going to tell me." She was smiling, and Rafe knew that was a good sign—a crack in her armor.

"A calculated risk is worth a thousand rash impulses."

"That sounds likes something Confucius might have said. But Rafe, about this check—"

"It won't bounce. In fact, if you're feeling really guilty about it, you can lose it at Atlantic City."

"About Atlantic City—"

"Here comes Carla. We'd better leave you to your other patients." He longed to reach out and touch her. He didn't. "Thanks for taking care of Scruffy. Oh, and how does a seven-o'clock flight sound for our Atlantic City departure?"

With a sigh that bordered on a laugh, Kat tossed her hands in the air. "You win!"

"Let's hope we both win."

"Win what?" Carla asked as she returned from the kennel.

"Buckets of money, sweetie. C'mon, Dr. Racanelli needs to get back to work."

Perhaps because the rest of the day was fairly uneventful, Kat's thoughts were never far from Rafe and all the confusion surrounding her feelings for him. She did have to admit that he cheered her up; this was odd, considering their initial encounter. Was it possible that it was only a week ago? And now she was flying to Atlantic City and God knows where else with the man!

As Kat had predicted, Scruffy's constitution helped pull him through surgery. Although he'd stay at the clinic until the end of the week, he was showing definite signs of improvement the following day. Unlike Monday, it was a slow day, leaving plenty of time for Kat to think and rethink the upcoming evening in Atlantic City. What on earth had made her agree to go? Undoubtedly her vulnerability to Rafe's deadly charm.

As soon as the clinic had officially closed, Kat ransacked her closet for an appropriate outfit for their gambling date. The red silk with rhinestone straps? No, she really didn't want that kind of attention. Seeing the turquoise lace made her laugh, but no, she'd pass up wearing it. Finally she decided on a mauve silk sheath with a mandarin collar. The slit at the side of the straight skirt was about as daring as she could handle for that evening. Jade teardrop earrings and a delicate matching necklace were her only accessories. Little makeup was needed; her color was heightened enough as it was, and despite her apprehension, her eyes sparkled.

When the doorbell chimed, Killer leaped off the bed, zoomed past Kat and raced down the stairs. He let out several passionate yowls, then plopped down before the door.

"You've made a friend for life," Kat said with a laugh as she let Rafe in. Then, retrieving her purse and coat from a nearby chair, she added, "If he had his way, he'd probably want to come to Atlantic City with us. Oh, by the way, he got into the kennels and has actually made friends with Scruffy."

"But they're both males."

"It's probably because Killer's neutered. Anyway, thought you'd like to know." With Rafe's help, she shrugged into her coat.

"Wonders never cease. I take it Scruff's still okay?"

"He's a real champ," Kat replied, looking up at Rafe. His hands were still lightly curled around her coat collar, and his breath softly ruffled the hair on the nape of her neck. Their eyes met and held. Blinking, Kat broke the spell, then fumbling in her purse, she retrieved the door keys.

"Ready if you are."

"Hey, that's a pretty grim face you've got on, Dr. Racanelli. This is going to be a fun evening. The weather's great for flying."

"I'll probably have my eyes closed, so it won't matter." Kat tried for a light response, but knew she failed utterly.

Rafe took hold of her shoulders, gently turned her toward him and said, "You don't like flying, do you?"

"Let's just say it's not my favorite mode of travel. Though it does beat balloons. Hey, I'm going to be all right, and I promise not to turn green."

Threading his arm through hers, Rafe said, "I'll bet you've never even been in a small plane, either."

"Nope. The 747s are bad enough."

"My Beechcraft Bonanza might make a convert out of you."

"Right," Kat murmured as they made their way to Rafe's car. "Next thing, you'll be teaching me how to fly."

"Not a bad idea, Half-Pint. That's one way to get over your fear of flying." Opening the car door for her, he softly added, "Might help some of your other fears, too." Seeing the startled look she sent him made him wish he'd kept his mouth shut. Getting her to open up to him was going to be a slow process. What did he really know of her? Nothing, absolutely nothing, except for the fact that she was a damn good vet and that behind her feisty facade was a frightened woman.

Settling in the bucket seat beside her, he clicked on the ignition, then headed down her drive to the road. He might not know much about Kat's past, but he knew how he felt about her. He knew he loved her, wanted to help her and could no more let her go than cut off his right arm. He'd never felt that way about a woman before. He didn't know when it had begun, but knew it would never end.

By the time they got to Hanover Airport, Kat was looking pretty pale. "Why don't you help me do the walk-around," Rafe said as he paused before the door of his plane.

"The *walk-around?*"

"Follow me," he said with a beckoning gesture as he ducked underneath the plane. "First, I check under the carriage to make sure everything's in place." Rafe had already checked out the plane that afternoon, but he felt Kat needed the assurance.

By the time he'd finished the check and had untied the plane, Kat seemed more at ease. After he'd taken his seat inside the Beechcraft, she climbed in, fastened her seat belt and gave him a bright smile.

"You've been flying long?" she asked in a conversational tone.

"Fifteen years. You think that's long enough?"

A tentative smile played on her lips. Then, pointing to the instrument panel, she said, "Are you going to tell me what all that equipment does?"

"Better still, once we're airborne you can take control."

"You're kidding, of course."

"Sort of," Rafe said, turning on the master switch. As the panel came to life, he reached over and patted Kat's hand.

"Wait till you see the lights of Washington, D.C., from nine thousand feet."

"My eyes are going to be closed, remember?"

"For fifty minutes?" With a chuckle, Rafe began to taxi toward the runway. "In case you do peek, the city will be on your left as we make our ascent."

"How high did you say we'd go?"

"We'll cruise at about nine thousand five hundred feet."

"*That* high?" They hadn't even taken off, but Kat felt something drop—her stomach probably. "Why are we just sitting here?"

"Waiting for our clearance from Richmond, and for that plane over there to take off." Rafe gestured toward a twin engine that had taken its position on the runway. His hand made a lazy circling gesture, then settled onto Kat's clasped hands.

"You knitting something?" His fingers curled around hers, then gave a gentle squeeze.

"Twiddling my thumbs. A nervous habit I picked up from my dad. It beats nail biting." As Kat gazed down at their hands, the fluttering sensation in her stomach increased. Just as her eyes flickered up and met his, he kissed her. Although it was like a whisper, soft and enticing, she felt as if they'd already taken off. Then he kissed her again. His mouth was slightly open and she tasted him, felt his tongue as it rubbed along her bottom lip. One of his hands went up and slowly sifted through her hair. It was an infinitely gentle gesture, yet it went straight through her like an arrow.

"This beats twiddling thumbs and nail biting, don't you think?" Even though Rafe had pulled back, the feel of his lips was still on hers. The touch of his fingers still ruffled her hair. And in the background there was the rumble of engines. "I think we're ready for takeoff," he said as the tower called with his clearance.

Kat nodded in agreement, then reclasping her hands, pressed herself as far as she could into the seat. It reminded her of all the scary movies from childhood when she would shiver down in her seat, clamp her hands over her ears and shut her eyes as tightly as possible. Of course, there was always a happy ending, and for that, Kat would emerge from her cocoon. But this was real life.

Suddenly the engine got louder, and the next thing she knew they were hurtling down the runway. Kat, much to her surprise, not only kept her eyes open, but kept her face practically glued to the window. She gulped for air as the plane ascended, then gulped again as it veered to the side.

"Everything all right?" Rafe asked in a loud voice.

"Fine!" Kat shouted back over the roar of the engine. Though everything was far from fine, at least she hadn't gotten sick, or worse—hysterical. Maybe Rafe was right; maybe after this trip, if she survived, she'd have her fear of flying conquered. Wasn't there a book by that title? she idly wondered.

"Once we level off, I'll let you drive, if you like," he said with a chuckle.

"Thanks, but I'll pass and just take in the scenery." *Fear*—what an ugly word. "You were right about the view, though," she said, interrupting her own thoughts. "Ashland looks like a fairyland."

"You've never seen a city from the air before?"

"On the evening news." Kat took in a deep breath, somewhat amazed that she was actually enjoying the view.

"Have you traveled much?"

"I went to Italy with my family when I was in high school, but that didn't count, because we went by ship. Then when

Jack and I were in Montana we flew back east pretty often. Saw a lot of movies that way."

"Jack?"

"My . . . my deceased husband." Kat's voice dropped.

"Oh. I'm sorry."

"It's been more than a year, so I'm . . . well, I *think* I'm on the mend. Though to hear my family talk, you'd think I never went out anywhere!" She rapped on the window. "If they could see me now!"

"Like I said, you need a little excitement. I've probably gone overboard with Atlantic City."

"My family will cheer. You see, they've been pretty worried about me. I suppose with good cause, because after Jack died—that's all in the past—yet they still think I'm living back then."

It was Rafe's turn to take a deep breath. Kat had let her armor down, and all of his protective instincts rose. It made Rafe love her all the more, yet he seemed at a loss for words.

Kat supplied them.

"In some ways, they're right. Jack and I were as close as this." As she held out index and middle finger, Rafe felt an irrational sense of jealousy stab through him. "We were both veterinarians, and I guess my identity was pretty much tied to his."

Rafe cast a sidelong glance at Kat. She was staring out the window and, though he couldn't see her eyes, the side of her cheek looked so soft and vulnerable. He wanted to ask more about Jack, but instead said, "You don't strike me as a woman who'd get lost in *any* man."

"I was younger then," she replied, turning her face toward him. After a pause, she slowly added, "There's more to the story, but now's not the time to tell it."

"Whenever you want an ear, I'm here."

"Thanks."

Reaching out, he stroked the side of her face. "In fact, right now I'm just listening because George is driving."

"George?"

"Automatic pilot. Easier than a car, once you get up in the air."

"But shouldn't your hands be on the wheel?"

"Automatic pilot gives you a lot of freedom." His hand made a lazy inventory of the nape of her neck. "So, if you don't feel like hitting the casinos we can circle Bater Field."

"I think you'd better get both hands on the wheel, or—"

"Yoke."

"Right. The yoke. I don't see any yellow dividing lines on Heaven's Highway."

"It's not as crowded as I-95, so we sort of watch out for each other."

"What about in fog?"

"We fly with instruments then. But tonight it's clear sailing." Rafe longed to reach out and touch her once again, but exercising restraint, he *did* manage to keep his hands on the wheel.

Gusty winds off the Atlantic Ocean made their approach to Bater Field a little rough. Kat tried closing her eyes, but unable to take the suspense, opened them.

"The water looks awfully close," she said, clenching her moist hands in her lap. "Is it always like this?"

"Before landing it better be. Oh, don't worry, we'll clear the bay. See, we're right on target."

"Oh!" Kat said on a gulp of air. "We're landing!"

"Touchdown! And we missed the big drink," Rafe said as the plane continued down the runway. Then, turning to Kat, he added, "Have a better feeling for flying now?"

"Well, I have to admit, I prefer it to the big birds," she replied, unfastening her seat belt. "Still, I'm not totally comfortable."

"Everything takes time."

"I know." Kat caught the look in his eye. There were determination and patience, and something else she couldn't quite put her finger on.

"So what's it going to be?" Rafe asked twenty minutes later as they entered Shangri-la City Casino. "Blackjack, roulette or one-armed bandits?"

Kat, craning her neck, stared up at the checkerboard pattern of crystal chandeliers that decorated the mirrored ceiling. "I'm sorry, what was that?"

"What do you want to play? Blackjack, roulette—"

"If it's all the same, I'd just as soon watch all the little old ladies." Pivoting around, she added, "This is a fascinating place to watch people. But you know what's really amazing is that it goes on nearly twenty-four hours a day."

"You've never been to a casino before, have you?"

"Guilty as charged. So, give me a grand tour."

"Hey, did I say I was an expert on these places?"

"You came here like a homing pigeon, Sinclair. C'mon, you said I needed a little excitement, so excite me." Shrugging her shoulders, she quickly added, "You know what I mean."

"I'd hoped the excitement part was a given." Reaching down, Rafe took Kat's hand. "As for the grand tour, I've never been to Shangri-la, but they're all pretty much the same. Money, cards and high hopes. The American way."

"So let's go to your favorite table—you play and I'll watch."

"It's a deal," Rafe said, tugging on her hand as they pressed their way through the crowd.

For the next two hours, Kat sat semispellbound as Rafe won more than six-hundred dollars at the blackjack table. From there they hit a roulette wheel where he won a hundred, then lost a hundred.

"Time to go, I'd say, wouldn't you?" Rafe patted his wallet, then carefully tucked it away in his sport-jacket pocket.

"Aren't you going to try to win it back?"

"If I didn't know better, I'd say you were a hardened gambler, Dr. Racanelli. C'mon, it's getting late."

"But you were winning at blackjack."

"And that's the time to fold up." Taking her firmly by the arm, he added, "What do you say to a bite to eat before we head back?"

Rafe chose an intimate restaurant with a candlelit atmosphere and view of the ocean. Their lobster dinner and chilled white wine were accompanied by the faint strains of classical piano.

"You know," Kat said, allowing Rafe to refill her wineglass, "I'd never have thought Atlantic City would have a restaurant as low-keyed as this."

"Life is full of surprises," Rafe remarked, watching the brandy-colored lights in her luminous eyes. "For instance, I'm surprised you didn't tell me sooner that you'd been married." He wanted to reach out and touch her hand. Instead, he took a sip of wine.

"I hardly ever talk about it...."

"Forgive my intrusion." Rafe did touch her hand this time. It was smooth and dainty, and it made him want to protect her from further pain. "Sometimes," he added slowly, "I bungle in where saints would fear to tread."

"It's really all right. Besides, maybe it would help me to talk a little about it." Although Kat averted her glance, Rafe noticed the flicker of pain in her eyes before she looked back up at him.

"More than a year ago my husband was killed in a stable fire." Expelling her breath as if having confessed a sin, she slowly added, "We'd been out cross-country skiing. It was one of those crisp, cold Montana afternoons when everything seems so vibrant. Jack and I had been out for several hours, and were on our way home when we smelled the smoke. By the time we saw it, it was really too late." In the pause that followed, Rafe watched Kat's eyes glaze over with memory.

"But when we heard the whinnied cries of all those trapped horses, Jack insisted on going in to save them. I tried to stop him . . . I really did. . . ." Rafe felt the pressure of Kat's fingers as they entwined with his, felt the tension ripple through her. "But I failed," she added in a whisper. "I failed and Jack died."

"I'm sorry," Rafe heard himself say. He groped for something more effectual, but he'd never been much for platitudes. Cradling her hands between his, he added, "I can't imagine you failing anyone."

"I did." Her lips trembled. "I was unable to stop him."

"You're not to blame," Rafe said, stroking her hands gently.

"Logically, perhaps. But I keep wondering if there wasn't something I could have done. You see . . . he went into the burning building and never came out." Unshed tears glistened on Kat's lashes. Withdrawing her hand from Rafe's, she dashed the tears away. "If only I could remember what happened."

"*Remember?*"

"That's the worst part of it. The last thing I recall is standing in front of the burning stable calling Jack's name." Her eyes flashed up at Rafe's. "I was terrified for him, but I couldn't move. I passed out, and the next thing I knew I was in the hospital being treated for shock and exposure."

"I suppose if I told you you were being too hard on yourself, you'd tell me to mind my own business."

"Never that." With a bittersweet laugh, Kat added, "The doctors say my memory *will* return, although I'm not sure if that's such a good thing."

"You're borrowing worry."

"I know. It's just that the worrying part gives me something to do."

"As if you're not busy enough," Rafe said on a purposeful chuckle.

"It keeps the confusion at bay," Kat replied with the beginnings of a smile. "But, really, thanks for listening."

"I'm always here for you. You know that, don't you?"

"Yes." Her voice was soft, almost unrecognizable to her. He was still holding her hand and, although the lightness of his touch sent soothing pleasure through her, it couldn't dispel the doubts that shrouded her memory.

And yet when he smiled at Kat, something turned over inside her, and as much as she wanted to deny it, she knew she was falling in love with Rafe Sinclair. Correction—she *had* fallen in love with him, and it scared her. She wasn't ready, knew she wasn't ready, couldn't be ready—not until she remembered what happened that night. Maybe then she could get a handle on her emotions. Maybe then she would be free to love again.

It wasn't until Kat got home that evening that her uneasiness sorted itself out into something concrete: guilt. She also knew her attraction to Rafe was real, and yet so was her fear of not only involvement, but of feeling vibrantly alive for the first time in more than a year. And her guilty feelings went back to Jack and the fire. What right had she to feel this good, to enjoy life this much after what had happened in Montana? Yes, Kat felt guilty all right—guilty for what she couldn't even remember. As long as she was busy at the clinic, those feelings were held at bay. But being with

Rafe tonight was such a vivid contrast to her everyday life that all her guilt had come to the forefront.

Her final thought as she drifted off to sleep was that she just didn't have the right to that kind of happiness. At least not yet. Not until she could remember those final moments of the fire.

The balmy weather continued the following morning, although forecasts predicted a cold front would move into the Richmond area that weekend, with temperatures dropping from the mid-sixties to the twenties.

Kat, taking advantage of the weather, had just opened all the windows in the reception area, when Rafe's red M.G. pulled into her driveway. Feeling her heart turn cartwheels at the thought of seeing him, she hurried onto the porch. Last night's spasm of recrimination was only a memory.

"Hiya, Dr. Racanelli!" It was Carla and a towheaded little boy in leg braces. He had an infectious grin on his freckled face, and from the way he wielded his crutches, it was obvious he didn't consider himself a victim of anything.

"I know it's kind of early and you've just opened, but we've come to check on Scruffy. Rafe's orders!" Carla put an affectionate arm around the boy. "Oh, and this is Stevie, one of Rafe's kids."

"Hi, Dr. Wacnell," the little boy mangled her name.

Digesting what she'd just heard, Kat opened the door and gestured them inside. *Rafe's kids? What* kids? Well, of course there was no reason why he wouldn't have children. It was simply odd that he hadn't bothered telling her. Perhaps he felt bad about the boy's infirmity.

"Nice to meet you," Kat said, sinking to the small boy's level and shaking his hand. "You like kitty cats?"

"All kinds!" he proclaimed, looking around the room. "Where are they?"

"Behind that door. Carla knows."

"We'll be right back, Dr. Racanelli." Then, as the teen ushered him into the kennels, Kat heard her say, "If it hadn't been for her, Scruffy would have died!" From all accounts, it appeared that Kat had become, as Rafe would say, one who walked on water.

But as for Rafe, just what was his story and where *was* he? How on earth did he think he could hide a small, crippled son? And why? But then, he'd sent the two children to the clinic.... Was he afraid to tell her in person? Did he think Kat would find his having a child offensive? Resting one hip against the receptionist's desk, she absently shuffled through the appointment book as if it contained the answers. Perhaps the courts had given his ex-wife sole custody, and allowed him only brief visitation rights.

An ex-wife? And all this time Kat had assumed he'd never been married. Well, that showed her how much she knew. How like a man. And to think, she'd apologized for not mentioning *her* marriage! At least she hadn't any surprise children to spring on him. So, Stevie was one of Rafe's kids. How many did he have, anyway? Five? Six? Of course she could just come out and ask Carla, but she'd probably think it a bit strange that Kat didn't know.

Further thoughts on the matter were interrupted as the teenager and the little boy burst into the reception room; Stevie, with his crutches flying out in front of him, looked like a contender for the Special Olympics.

"Take it easy, Stevie," Carla said in a very adult voice as she gently collared him. Then, looking up at Kat, she added, "Of Rafe's four kids, this one gets in the most trouble!" Then, giving the boy a hug, she said, "I'm just teasing!"

"I know," he replied, thoroughly enjoying the attention.

Kat took special care not to let her jaw hang open. *Four children?* Then, despite her best intentions, she blurted out, "And where is your Uncle Rafe's wife?"

Carla looked puzzled. "Uncle Rafe isn't married, never has been. But hopefully his status will soon change! Well, we'd better get back before he starts to worry. He wants to work with the kids this afternoon, and since they only come twice a week, it's pretty special."

After Carla and Stevie left, Kat sank into the receptionist's chair and tried to make sense from what she thought she'd just heard. *Unmarried, never been married, but gets his four kids twice a week.*

Chapter Nine

Even though Kat's day was full of back-to-back emergencies, the thought of Rafe as the father of four children was never far from her thoughts. By the time four-thirty rolled around and she'd treated her last cat, she decided to stop by River Run Farm and see the rest of his children herself. According to Carla, Rafe would be spending the afternoon with them.

Not being one who usually agonized over her wardrobe, Kat was annoyed with herself for trying on three outfits before deciding on a pair of jeans and a blue angora cardigan. A touch of blusher on her cheeks and a token dab of lipstick completed the ritual. Standing back for a look in the mirror, she decided she looked appropriately casual; children could relate to that.

Slinging her purse over her shoulder, she headed out the door. *Four children.* Kat had always loved children. She and Jack had planned to start a family once their careers were established. They had even decided on their first son's name—John Harley—in honor of Jack's motorcycle and the day Kat fell in love with him.

But there had been no children. Time and fate had crept up on them and snatched their dream away, leaving nothing but ashes to mourn.

Kat's fingers tightened on the steering wheel as she turned onto Blacksmith Lane. She knew she could never take such a loss again—the pain would be too much. Yet what would she have if she continued to live in the vacuum of her work? Success? Yes. Gratitude of her clients? Again, yes. In time, she'd even have financial security. There was always the satisfaction of caring for the animals. But what about her heart? What about those dreams of having her own family? Wasn't there an old cliché about the patter of little feet?

The thought of Rafe as father to four children seemed so out of place. Not that he wouldn't be a fine father, but somehow... Why hadn't he told her?

These thoughts were set aside as Kat pulled into Rafe's driveway. Carla, Stevie and three other children greeted her. They all wore riding helmets and carried small leather crops. Kat didn't have time to wonder about them. In fact, she'd barely gotten their names straight before Rafe and his tall blonde companion appeared.

"Dr. Racanelli!" He waved to Kat as if nothing were out of the ordinary! Then closing the distance between them, he introduced her to Gwendolyn.

"She's practically a second mother to them," Rafe said proudly. "I guess Carla's told you all about the program and how lucky the kids are to have Gwen."

"Hey, Rafe, these are your kids," the blonde said, giving him a playful tap on the shoulder.

"Last year Uncle Rafe had only two here, and they both were walking within eight months! Can you believe that?"

"Two kids?" Kat repeated, digesting this bit of news. Perhaps he'd had *several . . .* well, not exactly wives, but . . .

"Of course, I was his first miracle child." Carla's chest swelled with pride.

"Just call me St. Rafael," he said, pulling on her braided ponytail.

At that point a chorus of "St. Rafael" arose from the children. The tallest girl, who held a cane and had a brace on one leg, turned to Kat and said, "We tease him a lot, but he doesn't mind." Then, nodding to the other children, she added, "We'd better get going. It was nice to meet you, Dr. Racanelli."

Somewhat taken aback by all this, Kat watched Gwendolyn and Carla help the four children into a van. A sign on the outside of the vehicle read Pineboro County Physical Therapy. She didn't know whether to laugh or cry.

Turning back toward Rafe and shading her eyes from the sun, Kat finally said, "So they're *not* your kids!"

Rafe blinked several times in surprise. *"My kids?* You thought these children were mine . . . that Stevie, Megan and . . ." His voice trailed off.

"Well, Carla said they were. I must say, I did wonder a bit at her assurance that you'd never been married."

"I haven't." A grin stole over his features. "Of course that would have made them illegitimate, and would have made me a bit of a cad."

Thrusting her hands deep into her jeans pockets, Kat mused, "I must admit I was having trouble picturing you the father of four. Although," she said, laughing, "I rather admired you for acknowledging them, even if you did decline to marry their mother."

"Good of me." Rafe grinned. "Why don't you come inside?" he added. "In fact, why not stay for supper—nothing grand, mind you. It's the cook's night off."

"Thanks, Sinclair. I am rather hungry. . .and curious."

"Understandably, Racanelli!" Feeling her next to him was about as close to heaven as any man could expect. She was warm and vibrant, and brought out a surge of protectiveness he'd never known before.

"How does grilled salmon sound to you?" he asked when they reached the kitchen.

"Divine!" She was staring up at the skylight cathedral ceiling. "You know, I really love your house. It's so airy, and yet warm and cozy." Making her way to the island counter, she eased herself onto a stool.

"Glad you like it. There are several things I'd do differently, if I were to redecorate." Taking the salmon steaks from the refrigerator, he added, "Steamed broccoli and potato salad from the deli okay?"

"Fine. Here, let me rinse that off," Kat said, reaching for the broccoli. "And if you'll let me at your icebox I'll whip up some hollandaise sauce that will spoil you for life."

"Be my guest . . . but what's this 'icebox' business?"

"Oh, my family has always called them iceboxes. The story goes that Nana used one until they stopped delivering ice." Depositing lemons and butter on the counter, she said, "Mama remembers the iceman real well. Where are your knives?"

Rafe gestured toward a drawer. "You seem pretty at home in here. I'm surprised you don't know."

"Give me a kitchen, a full larder, a knife and a few pans and I'm in business."

"I thought being a vet was more in your line," Rafe said, slipping the steaks under the grill.

"Let's just say cooking is a close second. It's an occupational hazard that comes with being born into a family of Italian cooks."

"This must be my lucky night."

"You're going to have to sing for your supper and tell me about those children." Wielding the knife like a practiced chef, Kat began slicing through the lemons. She paused long enough to smile up at him, and Rafe knew he could never keep anything from her. Somehow he knew that, unlike his ex-fiancée Millicent, she wouldn't find it tiresome that Rafe gave time to the disabled children.

"Where shall I begin?" he asked after a beat.

"At the beginning." Moving past him, she reached up for a saucepan; it was just inches from her grasp. "Shorties of the world unite!" she cried, jumping up to retrieve it, then placing it on a burner, she turned her attention to the ingredients on the counter. "Tell me why an apparent playboy and wealthy architect would take time out for those kids."

"Apparent playboy?"

"Apparent," Kat stressed, slowly mixing the lemon and butter into the saucepan.

"It won't be long till dinner. Think you can wait?"

"I'm the soul of patience. I always wait for a good story."

Rafe leaned against the stove and watched as Kat, lost in culinary magic, whisked the hollandaise to aromatic perfection. He'd noticed her winsome, perky looks at their first meeting. He'd sensed her rhythm when they danced, tasted the promise of passion when their lips met, and now he drank in her grace as she moved about his kitchen. There was an elegance about Kat that he'd missed. Perhaps he'd always assumed that only tall blondes were elegant. How wrong he'd been!

Rafe had been wrong about a lot of things in his life. Becoming thirty *was* a turning point. Mimi had been predicting his Saturn return ever since he left grade school. Maybe she was on to something after all. She'd certainly been right about Kat. God, Carla and Marty, too! They'd all been right.

He was pleasantly surprised when Marty informed them that he was having dinner with Tonia, and that Carla was going to the movies with a friend.

"I went ahead and lit the candles in the dining room," Marty buzzed in Rafe's ear as he headed out the door. "Don't let it go to waste."

"Don't let what go to waste?" Kat asked, setting the broccoli and hollandaise sauce onto the table.

"The food!" Rafe said, holding her chair for her. Good Lord. Marty and Carla had set the table with the Belgian lace cloth, Haviland china and the mother-of-pearl knives and forks. It looked more like a wedding feast than a simple dinner.

"Everything looks beautiful," Kat enthused, apparently oblivious of the excess. "And I'm starving! But tell me, do you have little gnomes who do your bidding?" She was inspecting the bottle of chilled Chardonnay that Marty had put in the silver wine bucket.

"Don't you remember? A whole army of them resides in the basement," Rafe replied as he took his seat. "Very good of them to uncork that wine, wouldn't you agree? Allow me to sample it."

"And if it's inferior?"

Rafe took a sip and said, "It isn't." Then filling their glasses, he added, "Here's to the many stories we'll share and to continued happy endings."

As their goblets touched, Kat said, "I'm still curious to hear how you became involved with all those children."

"It's really because of Carla and an accident that happened to her ten years ago." He paused, then slowly added, "She and her parents were sideswiped by a truck. Carla and her mother survived, but her father was killed on impact. It was pretty awful for a while. In fact, it took my sister several years to get over it. But it was even harder for my niece.''

Rafe sucked in a deep breath. ''Aside from a concussion, the doctors couldn't find anything actually wrong with her—yet she just couldn't walk. It was psychological. That was her way of handling grief. She and my sister spent a lot of time on the farm. Carla kept asking to go feed the horses. Then I got the crazy idea that maybe it might be good for her to ride. One thing led to another, and as strange as it seems now, we had a breakthrough. She was walking within three months.''

''That's wonderful! Did you have any idea that that might happen?''

''I'd heard about using animals to heal depression in the elderly, but horse therapy was something else. Since then I've learned that it's an entire field in itself. The results really have been miraculous.'' Taking a sip of his wine, Rafe gestured toward their untouched plates. ''The salmon is getting cold.''

''Oh, you're right. I'm sorry... I got so engrossed I forgot about eating.'' Kat took a quick bite of the fish, then added, ''Tell me how you started helping the other children.''

''I'm a noble guy,'' Rafe said with a wink, as he speared some broccoli and hollandaise.

''Seriously, how did you get started?''

''Best hollandaise I've ever had.''

''C'mon, tell me about it.''

''The hollandaise?''

''Your horse therapy business!'' Kat countered on a swallow of potato salad.

''Well, when I saw what it did for Carla, I talked with her physical therapist at the hospital and found out that horses have been experimentally used to help children with every-

thing from learning disabilities to muscular dystrophy."
Rafe watched as her face softened.

"How does it work?" Kat asked, taking another bite of
salmon.

"It's actually fairly scientific. Seems that the riding motion helps the child by making both sides of the brain work
in unison. There's a surprising amount of documentation on
it." Rafe, topping their glasses with more wine, added,
"Why the long face? It's all happy endings. Besides, these
kids give me something to do aside from designing homes
for the rich. Keeps me off the streets and out of trouble."

"Amen to that! But really, I am impressed. You've done
something really wonderful, don't you know that?"

"Are you trying to give me a swelled head?" Reaching
across the table, Rafe brushed the top of her hand. It was
incredibly soft, he thought—like a flower petal. God, how
he wanted her; wanted to feel the smooth length of her
against him. But he also knew not to move too quickly.
There was still that inner bridge of trust yet to be crossed.
Then, gazing into her eyes, he saw the familiar flash of sadness.

"A swelled head," she repeated after a beat. "When I
first met you that would have been a distinct possibility. But
your mask is off, Sinclair. You're just your average nice rich
guy."

Kat stared down at her plate. She hadn't really meant to
say that; the class barriers from her school days were gone.
Rafe *was* rich, incredibly rich. He belonged to the elite
group she'd always envied. She tried to convince herself that
when all their differences were leveled, they were simply two
people whose lives had intertwined.

She knew in her heart that, like Jack, Rafe was everything she'd ever wanted in a man. Although the timing was

off, she still needed him, wanted his touch. It was in his arms that she could briefly forget the past.

By the time they had finished dinner, Kat had succeeded in distancing herself so far from her painful past that when Rafe suggested they have a brandy by the fire in the library, she agreed. The way he draped his arm over her shoulder and drew her toward him made her feel as if she'd already had several brandies.

Settling into the cool leather of the chesterfield couch, Kat watched Rafe start up a roaring fire. Aside from two candle sconces in the entranceway, the fire was the only illumination in the room. Its leaping tongues of orange flame haloed Rafe as he rose slowly and moved toward her. Euphoria seemed to lift her into his arms. Heat spread throughout her body.

"Kat." His voice came in a whisper, followed by his lips on her lips. Tenderly, hesitantly, tasting her as if for the first time. His hands caressed her face, then lightly skimmed the length of her throat. The kiss deepened as his tongue slipped between her lips to the warmth inside. Warm, wet and fiery.

Kat's breath came in little gasps. She couldn't quite get enough of him. Her body arched into his as a shudder of surrender went through her. Then, returning his kiss with eager passion, she twined her arms around his neck.

Rafe's response was as immediate as lightning in a storm. He pulled her against him onto the couch. Spreading her beneath him, Rafe consumed her with kisses that felt like a shower of stars. Light dazzled her closed lids; her body trembled as his hands seemed to caress every inch of her. As he shifted onto his side, she felt his hand slip beneath her pullover and stroke her bare flesh. His kisses began a lazy circle around her face—cheeks, nose and each eyelid received a salutation. Something like a growl sounded deep within him as that same hand eased its way up her back to unfasten her bra.

"Kat...Kat," he murmured. She heard the snap of her bra and felt her nipples harden with anticipation. The feel of his nubby wool cable-knit against her skin aroused her even more. A little sob broke in her throat as both his hands whispered a touch across her nipples. Then, in a slow squeezing motion, they closed around her breasts.

Kat, cresting a wave of pleasure, let out a moan as Rafe claimed her mouth once again. At the feel of his hardened manhood pressing against her inner thigh, she wrapped one jean-clad leg around him.

"Damn," he muttered against the side of her mouth, "I'm not sure I can take much more of this." Pulling back, he looked at her. "Not and survive, that is." A low chuckle punctuated this remark. "However, I'm a glutton for punishment...so..." Lowering his head, he took a nibble out of her neck. His fingers unfastened the top buttons of her angora cardigan.

"Rafe...?" Kat tried to no avail to steady the breathlessness in her voice. When he roughly opened her sweater and lowered his mouth onto her breast, she felt every nerve in her body tighten, then suddenly go limp. He teased the nipple of one breast with his tongue, while he gently squeezed the other.

Releasing his hold, Rafe moved his hand down to the waistband of her jeans and gently tugged at the snap. All the while his mouth, which seemed to be devouring her with a hot, velvetlike intensity, pressed a trail of kisses around each breast, before dipping even lower.

Kat, achingly aware of her own arousal, tried to fight back her shameless welcome of this intrusion. Rafe pulled back her jeans zipper and slipped his fingers beneath the edge of her panty. Kat arched forward and dug her nails into his shoulders. She wanted this, and yet it suddenly seemed wrong. Irrational, insane perhaps. A protesting voice inside her steadily grew louder.

"Rafe, no! Please . . . I . . . I can't." Struggling to a sitting position, Kat pulled her sweater together. Fumbling with tiny pearl buttons, she tried to avert her gaze from his. She was sure that explaining the guilt and pain would only make it worse. How could she possibly expect him to understand something she didn't? Glancing up at him, she saw a face set in rigid lines, and a cold light in his eyes.

"What do you mean, *you can't?*" His voice was husky, and there wasn't a damn thing he could do about it. He felt like one of his horses at the starting gate—only there would be no race tonight. "If it's protection you're worried about, I—"

"It's not that . . . I just can't. Please don't ask me to explain. I . . . I can't right now, that's all."

"But you *were,* that is, *we* were. I thought it was pretty good." Despite the fact that Rafe wished he'd kept his mouth shut, he knew he wasn't finished. There was an ache inside him—and it wasn't just sexual longing. Damn! Why couldn't this woman be easier to get along with?

"It was good, very good," Kat said. "It's just that things got a little out of control."

"Maybe you'd be better off if things *did* get out of control! You've got too damn much control in your life anyway." Rafe hadn't felt this frustrated since he was a teenager and had to take cold showers. Hell, it would take a dip in a frozen pond to cool him down tonight.

"Well, maybe I feel differently about control issues than you do! It's undoubtedly been quite a while since a woman's turned down your advances."

"My advances! Is that what you thought all of this was? Advances? Don't you give me credit for anything?" Jamming his hands into his pockets, he stared steadily at her.

"Of course I do. You're a fine architect, you're..." Struggling with the snap of her jeans, she shot out, "You're...handy with your hands...your therapy for the children is...is..."

"Don't strain yourself," Rafe interjected, still feeling the sting of rejection. He wondered why he wasn't handling it better than he was. His rational mind battled with his instincts. He knew that something or someone had hurt Kat very deeply. So deeply that it made it impossible for her to let go. He'd wanted to comfort her, and instead he'd let his hormones call the shots. Right...that was real manly.

On the instinctual level, Rafe had reacted the way any normal red-blooded male would have. He'd cool down... eventually. However, Kat was another matter; she was as skittish as her name. Any false move on his part was liable to send her flying.

"I...I think it's time for me to be heading home." She clasped her hands behind her back and softly said, "The dinner was delicious, and...and thanks for telling me about Carla."

"The least I can do is see you to your car," Rafe said, moving toward her. "I still have *some* gentlemanly attributes left, despite my lapse back there."

"I didn't say I didn't like it," she said quietly.

"Glad to hear *that*," he said, feeling some of his good humor returning. This was just round one; he'd lost a battle, but not the war.

After she left, Rafe remained on his deck. Although the night sky was a blaze of stars, there was the smell of snow in the air. His Aunt Mimi had always said that a change in the weather brought a change in the heart. The only question was, in what direction was Kat's heart headed?

Seeing the lights on in her grandmother's house, Kat drove past her own cottage and headed up the long gravel driveway. There was no doubt about it, she needed counseling—astrological, emotional . . . you name it, Kat needed it. Guilt and fear jockeyed for first place in her scrambled thoughts. Despite Nana Rosa's flights of astrological fancy and matchmaking attempts, she somehow always gave good advice. Kat knew tonight would be no exception.

"Ah, *bambina mia!*" Rosa cried, enfolding her granddaughter in her arms. She gestured toward the parlor. "*Viene, viene!* I just finished your astrological progressions. Now tell me, where else can you get such good service?"

"And at this hour!" Kat interjected with a laugh, as she followed Rosa into the parlor.

"At any hour for you. Ah, and such a good forecast. Truly the stars are shining down on you."

"I knew you'd cheer me up."

"Always I do that, *sì?*" Placing her hands on her hips, she looked Kat up and down. "But you are much too pale. So, I pour you a glass of sherry and show you these progressions." She poured Kat a glass from a crystal decanter, then settled on the velvet love seat next to her and said, "Sip the sherry slowly, and all your dreams will come true."

"Dreams? I could use a few sweet dreams." Kat paused and fingered the small glass in her hands. "Nana, I've been having the nightmares again."

"*Dio mio!* No! This should not be happening." Snatching up the astrological chart that lay on the coffee table before them, Rosa jabbed her pudgy finger into it. "Saturn has finally moved off the square to this divine Mars/Venus in Libra conjunction. Do you know what this means?''

"Bliss?" Kat ventured as she took a sip of sherry.

"Very close." Edging forward on the sofa, Rosa slapped down the chart. "Saturn's lessons concerning your past are over. No more nightmares. Of this I am sure." Touching the rim of her sherry glass with Kat's, she added, "Tell me when these bad dreams started."

"About a week ago."

"After meeting the nice Rafe Sinclair?"

"Yes," Kat admitted slowly. "That's why I came to see you. You see, I'm...I'm..." She paused, feeling her cheeks grow hot.

"Attracted to him? Ah, *grazie a Dio!* But maybe you think it is wrong to be so attracted?"

"I'm...I'm... Oh, Nana, I'm so confused—"

"You love him—this I know—*and* you feel guilty because of what happened to Jack. But my *bambina,* you must put that memory behind you."

"How can I when there's no memory there?" As Kat slumped forward, Rosa put a comforting arm around her.

"Sometimes nature knows best. If you were meant to remember, you would. To put your life on hold is wrong."

"I'm going on with my life. I've got the cat clinic, and my family and . . ."

"And you are ignoring your heart. Without a heart, there is nothing. Without love, life is a desert."

"Nana, really." Kat couldn't help but smile at her grandmother. "I have a lot of love in my life. I have you and—"

"That's not what I mean." Rosa shook her head despairingly. "I'm talking about *amore,* you silly child."

"I won't die without it."

"No? Maybe your body will keep on, but your spirit will shrivel up."

Kat took a deep breath to hold back the unshed tears, then slowly she said, "I do care for Rafe, but I don't know what to do."

"Listen to your heart; it will tell you everything. Even Tonia finally listened."

"Tonia?"

"*Sì!* Your sister. How do you say in English? . . . the feminist! Well, she and Rafe's brother have become quite friendly."

"Oh, yes," Kat said with a smile. "They seem good for each other."

"Then you know about them?"

"News travels fast in this family. Nana, please, don't think that because Tonia is in love with Rafe's brother that I'm . . . that I'm in love with Rafe." Kat finished the sentence in a rush, then downed the last of her sherry.

"No matter how you fight your feelings for Rafe, it will turn out for the best in the end. The stars do not lie." Dreamily, Rosa added, "Your Moon on his Sun says it all."

"Promise me one thing, Nana."

"Anything, *bambina*."

"Don't send out the wedding invitations yet."

Rosa gave a little sniff. "When you all *do* decide to set the date, you will come to me for it, won't you?"

"Absolutely. We can't have any bad aspects now, can we?" At Rosa's triumphant nod, Kat could only wonder at how easily her grandmother had maneuvered her into saying that. She had come to her for advice, but surely there wasn't really anything to Kat's Moon being on Rafe's Sun, was there?

Chapter Ten

"Please, spare me," Rafe said with a sigh. He really didn't need this lecture. But from the way Marty, Mimi and his father were going on, it showed no signs of stopping. The cook had fixed lasagna for dinner and, although it was delicious, it made him think of Kat. But everything made him think of her—present company included. He hadn't seen her for twenty-four hours. It seemed like forever. His relatives seemed bent on reminding him of this fact.

"And furthermore," his father said, pushing his empty plate from him, "that girl isn't after your fortune."

"Small wonder," Rafe countered. "That business about me practically being an escapee from Oak Haven was going a bit far."

"I was simply testing the waters. You should thank me for it."

"Dad, I can test my own water if it's all the same to you."

"Is that what you've been doing with Kat this past week?" Marty asked as he scraped the last vestiges of lasagna from his plate.

"It's all going to turn out," Mimi chimed in. "It's in the stars. It really doesn't matter what anyone does."

"That must be why you brought us together," Rafe said, pouring his aunt more iced tea.

"That was different. People have to meet, or *nothing* gets off the ground." Accepting the glass of tea, she nodded graciously at her nephew. "Life isn't quite a fairy tale, and despite the fact that Kat practically seals herself in that clinic, I didn't imagine you riding up on a white horse to rescue her. Even Cinderella had to go to the ball to meet her prince."

"Prince Rafe," Marty drawled as he leaned back in his chair. "Does have a ring to it—wouldn't you agree, Dad?"

"Definitely." Sticking a pipe in his mouth, Barton struck a match, lit the pipe and puffed thoughtfully for a moment before adding, "Well, my boy, you have my blessing, *and* a word of advice—"

"Oh, leave the boy be," Mimi said.

"He needs advice at a time like this or else he'll lose her. I like that gal. She's got spunk, not one of those washed-out horse-faced debutantes—"

"Point taken." Rafe gave his aunt a wink, then turned toward his father. "Out with your pearls of wisdom."

"Having had two engagements and at least a dozen attachments, I think you could use a pearl or two!" Barton, pausing for dramatic effect, sucked on his pipe and said, "If you want the girl—and I know you do—go after her. Take a lesson from Marty and—"

"And get married several times?"

"Don't forget, old chap, I *was* divorced between nuptials," Marty interjected.

"I'll keep all this friendly interfering in mind," Rafe assured them. "But now, if you'll excuse me, I've got some drafting that can't wait—especially since we're due for an ice storm. Last time it knocked out my power for twelve hours."

"Oh, my heavens," Mimi said, rising quickly, "I'd best get on the road."

"I'll follow you," Barton said, getting out of his chair. "Well, Rafe, looks like we're deserting you. By the way, where's Carla? I thought she was staying here till her mother got back."

"She is, but tonight she's at a slumber party. Yours truly is going to be all alone."

"That's right," Marty put in, "because Tonia and I have plans."

"Spring is in the air," Mimi trilled as she slipped into her fur coat.

"With an ice storm on the way?" Rafe's eyebrows rose in a bemused expression.

"It will pass, it will pass," Mimi said airily. "With this nice Venus/Mars aspect, I have high hopes."

"Best kind to have," Barton agreed, as they moved into the hall toward the front door. No sooner had they reached it than a resounding knock was heard.

As Rafe opened the door to Kat Racanelli, Mimi murmured, "High hopes indeed!"

"Sorry to barge in on you like this," Kat began, wishing she hadn't come. "But Carla called and said you were lonely... that you missed Scruffy and—"

"For Pete's sake come on in. It's freezing out there," Rafe said, ushering her inside and closing the door behind her. "Scruffy is certainly welcome, but as you can see, I'm not exactly a hermit."

"Delighted to see you again, my dear," Barton said, extending his hand. "Can you forgive an old man's prankish behavior? You do remember meeting me at Rafe's birthday party, don't you?"

"Uncle Willy?" Kat asked with a laugh as she set the cat carrier down on a hall table.

"I was just concerned for Rafe," the older man began. "If you'd seen the kind of gold diggers he used to squire about, you'd understand."

"It's really okay," Kat assured him. "In fact, I thought it was very sweet of you."

"Well, I thought it was shabby," Mimi declared with a shrug of her fur-clad shoulders. "If he'd listened to me, that little charade would have been unnecessary. Uncle Willy, indeed!"

"No harm done is what I say. And on that note, I must be pushing off. Tonia and I have great plans for the evening." With a wink in Rafe's direction, Marty headed for the door.

"We're leaving too," Mimi echoed, as she linked arms with Barton. "I'm sure you two have a lot to talk about."

A protest was on the tip of Kat's tongue, but none of the parting guests gave her time to voice it. As the door closed, she merely said, "Scruffy has missed you."

"Thanks for bringing him by." A crooked smile lit up Rafe's face. It was the kind of smile that made Kat want to kiss him. Instead, a silence fell while they looked at each other. Scruffy broke it with an undignified yowl.

Kat quickly unlatched the cage and gently transferred him to Rafe's arms. "He's going to favor his right leg for about a week, but after that no one will ever know it was broken."

"Thanks, Kat." Rafe leaned over and brushed her lips with his.

"It was the least I could do. After all, I am a vet," she heard herself reply as his mouth closed over hers.

At Scruffy's protesting meow, Rafe stepped back and with a chuckle said, "He's jealous."

"If I leave now, the damage will be minimal," Kat managed to say, despite the fact that her whole body was on alert, that every nerve ending seemed to throb with need, and that she had fallen in love with Rafe Sinclair.

"Who said anything about leaving?"

"I just did. Besides, you and Scruffy need time together. He needs reassurance and love." As Kat stroked the cat's fur, Rafe brushed his fingertips across her hand.

"I suppose I should follow doctor's orders, right?"

"Right." Kat tried to pull her hand away, but Rafe captured it and dragged it to his lips.

"Healing hands," he said softly. After kissing her palm, he let it go. At Scruffy's renewed complaint, Rafe added with a laugh, "He thinks he's our chaperon."

"He's a very smart cat. He knows it's time for me to go, and time for him to have a late-night snack." Kat backed up a step, only too aware of the look in Rafe's eyes, only too aware of her heartbeat. "Good night, Rafe."

All the way home Kat felt as if a part of her were still with Rafe. The last time she'd felt that way was with Jack. But that was different, she tried to tell herself. Last night she'd dreamed of Jack and the fire—dreamed of it and wakened up in tears.

Somehow she'd made it through the day. She'd decided that Scruffy was doing so much better that it really was time for him to go home. Carla's phone call, though, helped her make up her mind. The only real surprise was seeing Rafe's father, aunt and brother. She had a feeling they'd been discussing her. Why was it everyone seemed so set on pushing her and Rafe together?

With a sigh, Kat pulled into her driveway. Tomorrow the clinic closed at noon and, with an ice storm on the way, she could retreat from the world and lose herself in a mystery novel. Hopefully tonight she wouldn't have the nightmare....

Mimi Chandler had just spoken to Rosa, who'd agreed that extreme measures were called for. Having spoken with her nephew earlier, Mimi learned that Kat had left almost immediately, and that Scruffy was doing fine. It was at this point that the idea struck her.

Dialing the number before she could change her mind, she waited impatiently while the phone rang. Finally, Kat answered and Mimi went into her act.

"Oh, Kat, thank heavens you're there! I just got a call from Rafe. Although he tried to make light of it, I could tell he was worried—"

"What's happened?"

"It's Scruffy. He's acting most peculiarly—yowling, throwing up and running in circles. I told Rafe he ought to take him to you immediately, but he said he didn't want to bother you, especially since you'd just left."

"It doesn't sound good."

Hearing the concern in Kat's voice, Mimi added, "And in the middle of our conversation his line went dead. So there's no getting through to him." Mimi hated lying, but there was a smidgen of truth to her story. She *had* talked with Rafe. The rest was fabrication.

The fact that he was going to turn his phone off so he could get some work done was all to the good. Kat was bound to try phoning and, not reaching him, she would feel compelled to check on Scruffy. All it would take was getting these two young people together under that divine Venus/Mars transit . . . and nature would take its course.

"I suppose I could go over there and check on him."

"Oh, that would be wonderful. You know how men are. Rafe will wait till the cat is practically dead before doing anything."

"I'm on my way!"

"Drive carefully, dear. You know we're due for an ice storm. Luckily, it hasn't started yet. You can make it to Rafe's and back before it's due to hit."

"Don't worry about a thing. I'll let you know how things turn out."

"By all means, do that," Mimi said with a smile.

After hanging up, Kat quickly tried Rafe's line. It was just as Mimi had said—no answer. Changing out of her nightgown into a pair of jeans and a pullover, she headed out the door. She couldn't imagine what was wrong with Scruffy, unless he was having a delayed reaction to one of his drugs.

During the drive back to Rafe's, she tried to figure out what could possibly have gone wrong. Unfortunately, the weather, fulfilling its promise, claimed most of her attention. A mixture of sleet, rain and snow cut visibility down to nothing. The winding country road was iced over, and more than once Kat practically drove into a ditch. Thankfully there hadn't been another car on the road.

By the time she turned onto Rafe's driveway, she was actually shaking. Even after three winters in Montana, she was still skittish about driving, walking or skating on ice.

The path to Rafe's door was well lit, but it was as slick as could be.

The expression on Rafe's face when he answered the door was something a little short of thunderstruck. The fact that he was cradling Scruffy in his arms, however, was a hopeful sign.

"Come in, come in," he said, moving aside. "I must say, though, this *is* a pleasant surprise."

"I came as soon as I heard. How is he?" Without further ceremony, Kat preceded Rafe into the living room. "Why don't you just set him down on the sofa next to me, and I'll check him out." Gesturing to a spot next to her, she opened her vet bag and added, "Mimi told me as much as she could, but you'll have to fill me in on the details. I want you to know it isn't just any cat who'd pull me out in weather like this."

"Are you feeling all right?" Rafe asked.

"Actually, I was about to lose myself in a murder mystery when your aunt called. On the drive over here I almost ran off the road twice. And since they're calling for more ice, I'd like to get this exam over as soon as possible so I can drive back while the roads are semi-navigable. Other than that, I'm feeling fine." After rattling all this out, Kat took a deep breath, then held out her hands for Scruffy as Rafe joined her on the sofa.

"Oh, so you spoke with Mimi...."

"She said you'd made light of **Scruffy's** condition," she replied, running her hands over the cat. "But he seems all right to me. How long did he run in circles?"

"Run in circles?"

Fitting her stethoscope in her ears, Kat listened to Scruffy's lungs and heart. Then, looking up at Rafe, she said, "Yes, running in circles. How long was he doing it?"

"If anyone is running in circles, it's me!" He laughed. "Scruffy has been curled up in my study for the past two hours. It wasn't until you knocked on the door that I even heard a peep out of him."

"He wasn't doing the throw-up meow?"

"The throw-up meow?"

"Yes. You know, that terrible yowl they do right before they throw up." Scratching Scruffy under his chin, she said, "Did you eat something that didn't agree with you?"

"He had some tuna and a bowl of water. There was no throwing up, yowling *or* running in circles. If I didn't know better I'd say my aunt had been hitting the bottle, or perhaps you—"

"Whoa! Sinclair. I was all ready for bed and a murder mystery. I did not imagine Mimi's phone call."

"Well, there's nothing wrong with Scruffy."

"So I see," Kat said, allowing him to spring onto her shoulder. "I also see that your aunt has gone overboard this time in trying to play matchmaker."

"What about your grandmother?" Rafe pointed out as he reached over and gave Scruffy a pat on the back.

"Nana, too," Kat conceded with a sniff. Giving the cat a kiss, she allowed him to leap from her arms onto the sofa. With eyes downcast, she began to idly stroke his fur. If she looked up at Rafe, he'd surely hear the thudding of her heart.

"Maybe they think we need a little help in the lonely-hearts department," he said after a pause.

"Well, neither of us exactly advertised, did we?" Kat felt as if she'd suddenly been stripped of all her defenses. "What I mean is," she continued, hoping her feelings weren't too apparent, "is that I am certainly not trying to make a match with you, or anyone else for that matter."

"But what if *I* am?" Rafe softly asked, as he lightly touched the back of her hand.

"Are you giving me warning?" Kat swallowed against the feelings that rose within her. He'd given her warnings all right—plenty of them.

"What do *you* think?"

"I think it's time I got going," she replied, rising to her feet.

"Seems we've been through this scene earlier," Rafe said. Then, reaching out, he gently traced the line of her cheek with his thumb.

"I'm not much for déjà vu."

"Then stay." He moved closer until Kat could feel his breath on her face, could smell the faint aroma of his aftershave. He moved closer still until the heat of his body was one with hers.

"I can't. The roads are going to be impossible if I wait much longer."

"Stay the night. I'll be the perfect gentleman. There are seven bedrooms. You can take your pick." His hand encircled her neck. Then with a slow, sensual touch he began to massage the area.

"I'd better not," Kat said, despite the tingling desire that spread through her like a fire, "there might be an emergency—"

"Which I'm sure you're prepared for. You've got an answering machine, and if I'm not mistaken, that's a beeper in your back pocket." Playfully, he gave her bottom a pat. After withdrawing his hand, Rafe solemnly said, "I promise, no more funny business."

"Right…because I'm on my way out. And then you can get back to work." Disengaging herself from Rafe, Kat started toward the door. Rafe snagged her arm and drew her against him.

"I wish you wouldn't go." His lips teased the corners of her mouth as he pressed against her again.

"I really have to," Kat heard her muffled reply as his mouth opened onto hers. Gently his tongue nudged past her teeth, then tentatively explored within, breaking down all of her defenses. She felt her breath catch as his hands slid beneath her coat, lazily straying to her buttocks. With a sudden roughness he pulled her against him. He lowered his head and softly nibbled her throat.

Her breath came in a gasp, but despite the powerful urgings, she managed to say, "I thought you said 'no funny business.'"

"Short-term memory loss," he admitted as he pulled back. "But is it my fault if you have that effect on me?"

"All the more reason to leave." Ducking past him, Kat added, "I've been told cold showers do wonders."

"They probably bring on heart attacks," he said, following her rapid stride to the front door.

"I think they're supposed to take your mind off pressing problems." Whirling around at the door, she said, "But thanks for the invite just the same."

"I'll walk you to your car."

Before Kat could protest, he'd claimed her hand and was leading her around to the side of the house. A light freezing rain sang off the flagstone path. "Keys, please," he said as they reached the vehicle.

"Oh, Rafe, really. I'm perfectly able to start my truck." Realizing he wasn't going to budge, she dropped the keys into his outstretched hand, then quickly climbed in the passenger side.

When the engine failed to turn over, Kat could have sworn she heard Rafe chuckle. "It's not funny, Sinclair!"

"How old is your battery?"

"I don't know. But you might try pulling out the choke."

"It's the first thing I did," Rafe said cheerfully. "I'd say you have a dead battery."

"And if I didn't know better, I'd say you were out here tampering with it."

"Maybe Mimi or Rosa put a hex on the truck," Rafe suggested as he turned the switch once again.

"Wouldn't surprise me."

"Mimi says we're a match made in heaven," he said, tapping the accelerator.

"I'm surprised you believe in the stars."

"Aquarians are full of surprises," Rafe said as he switched off the ignition and handed Kat the keys.

"You're not going to try it again?"

"It won't help, my love, because you left the parking lights on. Besides, it's colder than a witch's—"

"Oh, dear! I guess I don't have much choice but to stay." Kat felt her heart skip a beat at the thought of it. "So, lead me to one of those seven bedrooms," she said, opening the truck door and jumping down.

"Preferably the farthest from mine," Rafe teased as he reclaimed her hand.

Despite the snapping cold wind and the icy footing beneath her feet, a delicious sense of warmth spread through Kat.

"I'll put you in the southern exposure room. Hope you'll like it." As his fingertips brushed the inside of her palm, bubbles of excitement went off inside her.

"I'm sure it'll be fine," she replied as they entered the house. Reclaiming her hand, she added, "Do you really think it's the truck's battery?"

"Pretty sure. I could jump-start it tonight, but the roads have gotten pretty treacherous. It'll be better if we wait until morning."

"You're probably right," Kat agreed. "If you'll please direct me to the . . . southern exposure bedroom, was it?"

"Upstairs, hang a right and go to the end of the hall. In fact, I'll show you."

"No, that's okay. I think we've said our good-nights." Kat edged toward the stairs.

"The inside shutters are pretty tricky."

"I've closed shutters before. Maybe I'll even enjoy a view of the stars."

"I guess this is good night again," Rafe said as he leaned over and kissed her lightly on the mouth.

Kat knew she should pull away, but every fiber in her body wanted him to prolong that kiss—to deepen it. She ached for the taste of him, but it was he who pulled away.

"Until tomorrow then." His lips were inches from hers as he reached out and stroked the side of her face. "The Jacuzzi will take the chill out of you." Then, kissing her lightly, he backed away. His eyes smoldered with a dark blue fire.

"Good night again," Kat said, as she turned and quickly mounted the stairs. She could almost feel the heat from his gaze as it burned into her.

Like the rest of the house, her bedroom had arched ceilings fashioned of stone, wooden beams and glass. The shutters that Rafe had referred to were on an angle with a wall of glass that looked onto the orchard. Outdoor lighting glistened off the ice-spiked limbs of gnarled apple trees. The ground was a carpet of frost.

The central focus of the bedroom was a gossamer white canopy over a queen-size bed. End tables on either side of it held Tiffany-style lamps, whose multicolored light filled the room with a soft glow. It was almost as if everything had been waiting for her.

Shaking off what she was certain was a ridiculous sense of destiny, Kat crossed to the bathroom, thinking that a nice hot shower would set things right. She stopped short at the view of a sunken Jacuzzi surrounded by lush green ferns. Three of the walls were mirrored tiles, and the fourth, an arched stained-glass window.

With an unexpected sigh of pleasure, Kat filled the Jacuzzi with water. Slipping out of her jeans and pullover, she eased herself into the warm and bubbling water. Resting back against the rim, she allowed her thoughts to drift into oblivion, and to just feel the pulsating water as it massaged her. All the things she had worried about suddenly seemed so far away. Everything except Rafe. Rafe, whom she'd tried so hard not to love, had crept into her heart anyway.

Feeling the water lap softly across the tops of her breasts, she remembered his touch, remembered his lips as they encircled the nipples and sucked. How she'd wanted him! Wanted him inside her, all around her, as every nerve in her body cried out for his touch.

Sliding her hands across her breasts, Kat let out a shivering response. Her nipples hardened, as memory crested with pleasurable sensation and something in the pit of her stomach rippled in anticipation. Just the thought of Rafe making love to her was almost more than she could endure.

Getting out of the Jacuzzi, she quickly dried off and tried not to think of Rafe. However, when she returned to the bedroom and saw the blue flannel nightgown lying on the bed, an odd, fluttery feeling went through her.

Rafe. His name lingered on her lips as she pulled the nightgown over her head, then slipped between cool sheets. She'd known she was tired, but she hadn't expected to fall asleep so quickly. Nor had she anticipated the nightmare that shattered her fragile peace.

Chapter Eleven

It swept down on Kat like some avenging angel. She'd had nightmares before, but none like this one. At first she was certain she'd opened her eyes, yet the room had disappeared. There was no gossamer netting above her bed. There was no bed, only a sensation of a biting cold wind to her back and a searing heat in front of her. It was so hot her eyelashes were actually singed and her cheeks burned.

It was at that moment that Kat realized she was having the nightmare again—only this time something was different. Something physical was keeping her from entering the burning stable.

She couldn't move! Suspended in midair, she looked down on herself in the dream. It was vivid, more vivid than she'd ever remembered it.

Kat felt a surge of helplessness overcome her as she watched herself falter forward with arms outstretched against the blazing building. She was calling Jack's name while she frantically beat away the licking flames that came within inches of her. The misty snow that filled the air had no effect on the fire. The gusty wind out of the north only fanned the flames even more.

Jack was inside. She'd begged him not to try to save the horses, but he'd gone in anyway. Gone in, and not come out. The fire-truck sirens could be heard in the distance, but she knew they wouldn't get there in time to save him.

On a surge of adrenaline, Kat, hugging the ground, managed to get past the flames and into the building. Hearing Jack's voice and the whinny of panicked horses, she plunged headlong into a smoky stall. Black spots danced before her as acrid smoke seared through her windpipe and tears filled her eyes. The last thing she remembered doing was reaching out for support and connecting with hot timber. Fiery splinters filled her palm as she slumped forward.

As Rafe finished his brandy by the fire, he tossed around several rather *ungentlemanly* ideas. Damn, just the sight of Kat threw his fantasies into full throttle. And despite everything, he was pretty sure she wanted him, too.

Stretching his legs out in front of him, he closed his eyes, leaned back against the couch and indulged himself a little more. He could almost feel her silky skin beneath his fingers, breathe in her springtime fragrance and hear the passionate sound of her voice.

Rafe wanted more than that, though. He wanted, *needed,* that sense of full release that lay within the folds of her womanhood. He would take her slowly, beginning with a whispering kiss, the kind designed to drive them both out of their minds. Then he would skim the lightest of touches down her neck and onto her breasts. Sweet, nibbling and sucking kisses would follow the trail his fingertips forged.

And Kat, arched beneath him, would be unable to deny this final act of love.

Damn! Rafe, opening his eyes and sitting forward, spilled the remaining brandy. Heedlessly, he placed the snifter to one side, and plowed his fingers through his hair. While Kat was in the Jacuzzi he'd laid out one of Carla's nightgowns for her. Then he'd purposely returned downstairs, keeping temptation at arm's length. By now, Kat was probably tucked in bed, all toasty-warm from her bath.

Rafe rose to his feet and was headed for the stairs when a distant cry cut through the air, and then another. He took the stairs two at a time, and when he burst into Kat's room she was sobbing hysterically on the side of her bed.

"Kat!" He reached out for her. Drawing her to him, Rafe murmured, "It's a dream, just a bad dream."

"Terrible . . . terrible. I tried to reach him! I did, I did!" Kat's eyes were closed and she was trembling.

"Of course you did," Rafe said soothingly as he pressed a gentle kiss onto her forehead. "Of course you did."

"I . . . I . . . couldn't move. Couldn't do anything in my dream. But I saw what happened." As she burrowed into his arms, Rafe felt a swell of protectiveness overcome him. He would do anything for this woman.

"What happened? Maybe it would help if you told me," he carefully suggested, rocking her in his arms.

"The fire . . . stable fire . . . I was there." She held on to him as a child waking from a nightmare might. "I was so scared for Jack. He'd gone into the barn to save the horses, and I went in after him." Pulling back, Kat brushed away her tears. Slowly opening her eyes, she added, "All this time I'd been afraid to remember what I'd done . . . so afraid that I'd stood by and let Jack die in that horrible . . . horrible fire." Gulping for air, Kat sank back into Rafe's arms.

"Of course you tried to save him," Rafe said, stroking her head. "You're the bravest woman I've ever known."

"I didn't think so," she said, her voice muffled against Rafe's shoulder. "I couldn't remember, and so I started thinking that maybe I'd let Jack die. But I *did* try to save him," she repeated on a sob. "Tonight I saw it all in my nightmare, and for the first time I remembered what really happened. I saw myself go into the stable. It was so real." Looking up at Rafe, she added, "I could even smell the smoke and feel the heat. It was so hot, and I couldn't breathe. That was why I passed out."

"You're safe now. I'm here, Kat, and always will be," he said, kissing her gently on the cheek. Then, caressing the side of her face with his fingertips, he added, "It's going to be all right from now on."

"I think . . . I think you're right," she managed to say. "Maybe I'll be free to live—really live again."

"Of course you're free, and the nightmare is over," he whispered.

"I'd wanted to tell you about it before, but I just couldn't. You see, I was living in the past." A bittersweet laugh punctuated this. "But tonight the past finally caught up with me. Forgive me for taking so long to open up." As she looked up at Rafe, a wave of unnamed emotion curled through him.

"There's nothing to forgive," Rafe murmured, catching her hand to his lips. How on earth could he begin to explain to Kat how very special she was to him, and how he loved her? Somehow he knew everything was going to be right from now on. He and Kat were as well matched as any two people could be.

"You are a brave and wonderful woman," he said at last.

'Thank you.'' Her voice was choked with emotion. "I'm so grateful for the memory, and to know that I did what I did.''

Rafe just held her close, feeling her breathing and rapid heartbeat. He wished there was something more he could say. For once, the words didn't seem to come so quickly—which was strange, considering the depth of feeling he had for Kat.

"Still,'' Kat added, breaking the silence, "that first time we met I was terribly unfair to you...."

"If I remember correctly, I was the hard case, not you. A lot has changed since then. That is, I hope it has.''

"It has,'' Kat said softly.

Feeling the ripple of her breath, Rafe pressed a kiss into her hair. "I suppose you could say we've both changed. I know I have.''

"Yes, you have, though I can't say just how.'' Turning her face toward his, she smiled softly. "The raw material was there all along. After all, it's not just any man who'd take time out for handicapped children, much less let them ride his prize mares.'' Cocking her head to one side, she added, "You're right out of a fairy tale.''

"Guess I've just gone from toad to prince—but that might be stretching it a bit much. Although if anyone's kisses could do it, yours would.''

Lowering his mouth to hers, he brushed her lips lightly. Then with infinite care he claimed her mouth, nudging it open with his tongue, and tasted the honeyed sweetness within. Kat's body responded like lightning as her arms twined around his neck and she shivered against him.

A whimper of pure pleasure escaped her lips as Rafe's hands skimmed across the top of the flannel nightgown. Her breasts were full and promising against his hand, and his yearning shot through him with an impatience he hardly recognized.

He wanted to touch and taste her all over; to have her silky skin beneath his callused palms; to feel her warm breath against his neck; and to hear her whispered cries in his ear. He wanted to know the feel of her moving beneath him; to know her sweet surrender, hot and moist; to enter her and fill her. He wanted to take away any trace of pain she'd ever known. He wanted to memorize every inch of her so that he might recall and savor it when they were apart.

But most of all, he simply wanted to love her. To love her with every fiber of his being—the way she was meant to be loved. How he had waited for this moment. He could only pray she loved him half as much. The past that had held her back now freed her for love, and hopefully freed her for him. But not yet...not like this. She was too open, too vulnerable. It was too soon.

"Rafe..." She whispered his name as he drew back. Rafe heard passion in her voice. It was all he could do not to drag her against him once again. As her hands flew up to his face, their caressing touch sent spirals of pleasure coursing through Rafe.

"Kat, you must know how much you mean to me...." He paused, startled at the roughness passion had brought to his voice. How could he possibly express what he felt? Words weren't coming, only the need and desire. He'd never met anyone like Kat before, and it just kept amazing him. She was everything he'd ever wanted, and yet he'd had to almost fall over her to discover the fact.

He was kissing her again, and feeling her pliancy against him took his breath away. Their hands tangled in an intimate dance between them. Pulling his lips from hers, his mouth descended to her hands, nibbling and kissing each finger. Forging a hot trail with his mouth down her slender arm, he pushed the flannel sleeve back to her shoulder. Then drawing her against him once again, his mouth dipped to the scallop-edged neckline.

Kat felt a shudder go through her abdomen, then slowly crest to her breasts. They were peaked and aching for Rafe's touch. He touched them and a ripple of desire swelled within her. He growled something in her ear as both hands encircled her breasts and stroked and squeezed them. When he unfastened the front of her gown and lowered his head, he took her nipple in his mouth. Kat let out an audible gasp and sent her fingers through his hair, holding his head to her as wave after wave of pleasure washed over her.

The nightmare and all its pain were completely obliterated. Kat felt her body melt and surrender beneath him. She was only dimly aware of the crackle of sleet against the window. All at once there was the sound of a sudden boom. Kat's awareness jolted forward.

Rafe shifted position and, with both arms propped on either side of Kat's head, he said, "Looks like our guardian angels are looking out for us...."

"Was that a celestial trumpet?" Kat asked. Her hands had strayed to Rafe's muscular chest.

"More like a power failure. That sound you heard was the breaker. Unfortunately my generator burned up last year, so I'm afraid it's going to get a little chilly in here unless I stoke up the fire." Leaning down, he gave her a quick kiss on the lips before pushing off the bed.

Pulling herself to a sitting position, Kat watched for a moment as Rafe crumpled newspaper and stacked kindling. Then she joined him by the hearth.

"These look pretty dry," she said as she handed him several medium-size logs.

Reaching over for the tongs, Kat prodded the logs. "For a while after Jack's death, I couldn't get anywhere near fire."

Rafe rose slowly. The guarded look on his face prompted Kat to reach out and touch his cheek. "I'm all right now, and have been for several months." Clasping her hands in front of her and staring into the flames on the hearth, she added, "Tonight seemed to bring everything full circle. I guess I don't have need to run anymore." She shyly looked up at him.

"I'm glad to hear that. Kat, you need never run again. You're home now." It was Rafe's turn to reach out, and sifting his fingers through her hair, he closed the space between them. "At least, I hope you'll think of this as home, if that's not being too presumptuous of me. What I mean is, you can still keep your cottage and the cat clinic.... No, that didn't come out right, did it?" With a chuckle he kissed her forehead. "Oh, brother, do I ever sound like a macho he-man...giving you permission to keep your place! You can sock me, if you'd like."

"Rafe Sinclair," Kat began, drawing away from him, "I'm surprised at you! All these years of being a sought-after bachelor...and you're tongue-tied now?"

"There's a first time for everything," Rafe said, looking slightly miserable. "And I am having trouble getting this out." He raked his fingers through his hair, then, resting an elbow against the mantel, added, "You'd think I'd have the hang of it, having done it once before."

"You'd think so," Kat agreed, biting down on a smile that threatened to erupt into a ludicrous grin. He loved her, she knew it. And unless she was mistaken, the man was trying to propose marriage to her. If she didn't do something, they'd probably be there all night. Despite women's lib, there was still something jarring about a woman proposing to a man. "Some people are just a little slow."

"I never used to be—"

"Oh, so it *was* the fast lane—jets and all that money can buy—after all!"

"That was in my past." Looking steadily at Kat, he said, "As hokey as it might sound, you seemed to come along at just the right time. You've helped me to change. Really, you have."

"And you've done the same for me," Kat said softly. "*And,* I'm glad you don't mind if I keep my cottage." Reaching out, she drummed her fingers against his chest.

"That was awkwardly put. Just delete it—pretend that I didn't say that." Closing his hand around hers, he added, "You must know how I feel about you...."

Kat swallowed. She *hoped* she knew how he felt about her. Yes, of course she knew! "Well," she began, "our first encounter was pretty memorable—"

"Delete that, too!"

"What do you think I am, a computer?" she asked with a laugh.

"Anything but."

"Of course, there was Nurse Racanelli with her strange herbal brews—"

"Which worked, I might add."

"Don't forget Hostess Racanelli...Dr. Racanelli with all those cats. Then there's my family...."

"I love your family—they're as zany as mine. Look at Dad." Rafe moved closer to Kat, and pressing his forehead to hers, said, "At least your family hasn't declared you unstable and relegated you to Oak Haven."

"Does this mean I'm going to marry into a family of—" Kat bit down on her lower lip.

"Crackpots? Possibly." Rafe pulled back and raised an eyebrow. "Hey, who said anything about marriage?"

"Delete it," Kat replied, feeling a hot blush slap her face.

"What do you think I am, a computer?" Rafe's hands trailed down her neck. He was smiling in a way Kat had never seen before; or maybe it was a trick of the firelight. The flickering orange light could do strange things, but surely it couldn't account for the wonderful warm feelings that sprang up between them. Being in his arms was the most natural thing in the world. She was meant to be there. Her past was truly healed, and Rafe was her present and future.

"Are you usually so forward with men?" Rafe asked, as his lips descended to the hollow of her neck and took tender nibbles.

"Only when provoked," she replied a little breathlessly as her hands once again wrapped around him.

"Well, what's your answer?" he murmured in her ear.

"My answer?"

"Will you?"

"Keep my cottage and the cat clinic?" Kat managed to ask as Rafe kissed her ear.

"Umm, that too."

Pushing away from him, Kat said, "Since this is undoubtedly one of the world's longest marriage proposals, I should probably be equally long in getting back to you... that is, if this *is* a proposal?"

"Hey, no fair." Rafe tilted her chin and gazing tenderly into her eyes, said, "It wasn't that long a proposal. And yes, that's exactly what it is."

"Really?" Kat's heart did a somersault in her chest.

"Is it so remarkable that I want to marry you?"

"Well, I'm not really part of your world."

"Thank God!" Pressing her hands between his, he added, "That's part of your charm. I don't know where to begin in telling you how special you are to me. I have no idea how it happened in such a short time, but I feel as if we've always known each other." His lips met hers in a soft kiss. "Always loved you. I can't begin to imagine my life without you. You see, you crept in when I wasn't aware. At first I tried to chase you out, but that didn't work."

"Oh?" Kat took a breath. "Sure you don't want someone a little more sophisticated?"

"Positive!" Rafe cupped her chin and kissed her again, then, on a laugh, added, "Kissing you seems to be the only thing that keeps you quiet. If I wanted sophistication, I would have married Millicent. You're the one I want."

"I...I just wanted to make sure. This seems too good to be true."

"More kissing is needed," Rafe said, lowering his mouth to hers.

"I might become addicted to this," Kat managed to get in, "and then when you're not around—"

"I'm always going to be around. Just try getting rid of me." He started to kiss her again, then said, "There isn't someone else, is there?"

Kat let out a gurgle of laughter as she snuggled into his arms. "Yes! Yes, I confess. But you already know how possessive Killer is."

"Killer?"

"You remember your allergy...."

"It was a cold—"

"I thought you never got sick."

"Okay, okay...I admit it—I do occasionally get sick."

"Lucky for you I know all these neat herbal remedies. But about Killer—we are sort of a package deal."

"Nice package," Rafe murmured, dipping in for another kiss.

"But you'll have the best lasagna and spaghetti in the world. I'm *so* modest, but then that's a Leo for you." Kat couldn't help grinning up at Rafe. How on earth had she gotten so lucky? Maybe there *were* still miracles. Perhaps love *could* triumph. She already knew its healing powers, and somehow she sensed that with Rafe her life would be complete and filled with that miracle of love.

"You still haven't given me an answer," Rafe prodded.

Kat felt as if her heart were going to knock clear through her chest. He was so close that the heat from his body warmed her, and she longed for that heat and his touch. How she longed to love him and for him to make slow and passionate love to her. She only had to say yes to ecstasy. Rafe was a man who knew what loving a woman meant. Once again, Kat bit on her lower lip to still the grin that teased her lips. Nana, after doing his astrology chart, had said that Jupiter in his eighth house would bring bliss to the marriage bed!

"Earth to Kat." Rafe was stroking her neck and looking very intently at her.

"Yes, of course I'll marry you!" Kat said, looking up at him through dewy eyes. "Though I can hardly believe it."

"Believe it," Rafe assured her, as his hand stroked the side of her face. "Also know that I love you, and I'm going to keep on loving you as long as you'll let me."

"That'll be forever," Kat said, allowing him to pull her against him. Her next words, muffled in his embrace, caused him to cup her chin and ask her to repeat herself.

"I love you." Her eyes teared. "I love you," she repeated softly. "I hope that's enough."

"Love is always enough," Rafe said on a kiss that went from head to toe and left Kat shaken but filled with a warmth that surpassed the fire on the hearth. It was the kind of warmth that would last a lifetime.

Epilogue

"*Viene, viene!*" Rosa cried, as she gestured to the photographer to get in place. "Now, when my granddaughter throws the bouquet, that's when I want the picture taken. She's going to throw it any minute!" Hurrying over to where Tonia stood, Rosa said, "Stand in front, you are *famiglia!*"

Tonia nodded and stepped forward. A sudden chorus of exclamations sounded as Kat appeared at the landing of her grandmother's curved staircase. In a single well-aimed toss, Kat practically hurled the bouquet at Tonia, who good-naturedly caught it. Marty, who'd been on the sidelines, quickly pulled her into one of the side rooms. The grin on Rosa's face was like a neon sign—it positively glowed.

"Now one more picture with everyone," she instructed the photographer as she put her arm around Kat. She beckoned for Rafe, Barton and Kat's parents to join them. Although she'd tried to get Mimi to join them, she chose to remain on the sidelines and cheer them on.

After the last photo was taken, Kat came up and gave her grandmother a hug. "Thanks for the reception. It was great, especially on such short notice."

"I do not believe in long engagements. Three weeks' time is plenty. And such a beautiful wedding, with that nice Venus aspect. It couldn't have been better!"

"Well, you chose the date," Kat reminded her with a laugh.

"One can't be too careful with these matters, although ten o'clock in the morning is a bit early—even for me," Rosa said. "Marriage is one of the most important steps you'll ever take in life. You got a good man and a good date to marry him. I predict success. Don't you agree, Mimi?"

"Since we were partners in crime in getting these two people together, I think I would agree." Mimi gave a pat to her upswept hair.

"Well, it worked," Kat said. "Although I didn't go down the aisle in reams of white satin, I've now got a new cocktail dress." Impulsively hugging Mimi, then Nana, Kat added, "I better say goodbye to the rest of the family or we'll miss that plane."

"I can't wait to show you what I've discovered in Kat's progressions and transits!" Rosa said later that afternoon as she rummaged through the stack of astrology charts that she kept in the bottom drawer of her desk.

Mimi squeezed some lemon into her tea. Then, smiling up at her friend, she said, "Well, I know you said that horrid square from Saturn to her nice conjunction of Venus and Mars was finally letting up. Is there something else?"

"Indeed there is!" Rosa said triumphantly as she sat down opposite her friend. "Take a look at that! Moon on the Sun. But here's the best news of all—transiting Jupiter on her Mars—all next year, and you know what that means...."

"A baby. Oh, that *is* splendid news." Mimi adjusted her glasses for a better look. "From the looks of things, it goes back and forth over that degree. So, it could be really any time."

"That's where we come in. Ah, *que divino!*"

"Oh, but Rosa, don't you think that's taking it a bit far? I mean, it's one thing to plan their wedding date, but the arrival of their children?"

"*Cara* Mimi, it is our duty! We are *la famiglia. È molto importante.*" Pouring herself a cup of tea and dropping several lumps of sugar into it, she added, "Drink up, we have our work cut out for us. Just imagine, a little Pisces baby with a grand trine. Oh, I do love having a project...."

* * * * *

LOVE AND
THE AQUARIUS MAN

by Wendy Corsi

February is traditionally a month for hearts and flowers, but the eccentric Aquarius man isn't about to rely on old-fashioned trappings to say "I love you." This imaginative fellow will search endlessly for the most *un*conventional way to romance his lady, and he'll enjoy every minute of it! He loves a quest, and he won't hesitate to browse through every store in town to find just the right gift... for just the right woman.

Rafe Sinclair, hero of *The Kat's Meow*, would surely delight Leo Katrina Racanelli with a basketful of cuddly kittens. What special Valentine would an Aquarius man give to you?

The *Aries* female enjoys a challenge—and she's got one when she sets out to win the heart of the free-spirited Aquarius male. Luckily, her go-get-'em attitude and amazing endurance will captivate him. On Cupid's day, the en-amored Aquarian can convince this possessive woman he's hers for eternity... with diamonds.

Can conventional *Taurus* and wild-at-heart Aquarius possibly live happily ever after? Yes—if he tones down that quirkiness...and if she learns to tolerate his occasional lapses back into eccentricity! He would be wise to forgo creativity when February fourteenth arrives...traditional Taurus will be tickled over a customary heart-shaped box of chocolates.

The *Gemini* lady and the Aquarius man seem made for each other! They're born explorers who love to discover all life has to offer. But they often get so caught up in their individual pursuits that they start to drift apart. This Valentine's Day, these soul mates should hop a plane to somewhere exotic and spend a whirlwind weekend doing everything there is to do...together!

Happy *Cancer*-Aquarius couples prove the familiar theory about opposites attracting. After all, she's an emotional homebody, and he's a casual wanderer. But true love has a wonderful way of neutralizing even the most drastic of conflicts! Besides, the Aquarius man knows just how to appeal to his Cancerian lady's beauty-loving nature. The perfect Valentine? An exquisite watercolor by her favorite artist, of course!

The *Virgo* woman and Aquarius man are such good friends that outsiders might find it hard to believe they're lovers, too. They can learn a lot from each other: she's organized and detail-oriented, while he's committed to altering the big picture. The Aquarian man appreciates the pride the Virgo woman takes in her appearance, and he'll thrill her this February with a day of pampering at the best spa in town!

Like the Aquarius man, the *Libra* woman finds joy in people, parties and spending money! Their joint bank account is probably empty most of the time, but neither really seems to mind as long as they're having fun. This Valentine's Day they'll enjoy nothing but the best—a chauffeured limousine, champagne and dancing till dawn in the best nightclub in town.

The *Scorpio* lady is passionate; he's merely affectionate. She's temperamental; he's as easygoing as they come. What *do* Scorpio and Aquarius see in each other? Plenty, when he forgets about saving the world and concentrates on her. There's nothing a sexy Scorpio woman would rather have on the most romantic day of the year than silky lingerie, exotic perfume . . . and private time with her Aquarius man.

Both *Sagittarians* and Aquarians value their individuality so highly it's amazing they've formed a partnership at all! But this fun-loving, sociable pair are destined for a happy life together—surrounded by their many friends. This Valentine's Day the Sagittarius-Aquarian duo will throw an enormous masquerade ball and invite everyone they know to come dressed as famous lovers from the past!

Neither *Capricorns* nor Aquarians are particularly emotional, but they understand each other perfectly. The often pessimistic Capricorn woman can be cheered by her Aquarian's frequent look-on-the-bright-side pep talks. She's a true romantic; he's a little less traditional. But an Aquarian man can liven up a quiet Valentine's dinner for two by hiring a trio of strolling gypsy violinists to serenade her!

When the Aquarian man gets together with the *Aquarius* woman, their love is bound to change the world. Those two are happiest when they're helping other people. February fourteenth won't find these two sharing a cozy hideaway. They'll be out celebrating their love at a glittery charity ball!

The *Pisces* lady dreams of being swept off her feet; the Aquarius man considers himself carried away if he pecks her cheek in public. But once they're hooked, these two aren't going to stray, and that's important to them both. The Aquarius man will thrill his nostalgic woman on Valentine's Day with tickets to a romantic movie...and sharing popcorn in the back of the balcony!

* * * * *

NORA ROBERTS

Love has a language all its own, and for centuries, flowers have symbolized love's finest expression. Discover the language of flowers—and love—in this romantic collection of 48 favorite books by bestselling author Nora Roberts.

Starting in February, two titles will be available each month at your favorite retail outlet.

In February, look for:

Irish Thoroughbred, Volume #1
The Law Is A Lady, Volume #2

In March, look for:

Irish Rose, Volume #3
Storm Warning, Volume #4

Collect all 48 titles and become fluent in

THE LANGUAGE of LOVE

LOL292

From the popular author of the bestselling title
DUNCAN'S BRIDE (Intimate Moments #349)
comes the

LINDA HOWARD

COLLECTION

Two exquisite collector's editions that contain four of
Linda Howard's early passionate love stories. To add
these special volumes to your own library, be sure
to look for:

VOLUME ONE: *Midnight Rainbow*
                  Diamond Bay
                  (Available in March)

VOLUME TWO: *Heartbreaker*
                  White Lies
                  (Available in April)

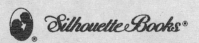
Silhouette Books®

SLH92